CONTENTS

PART FIVE
BACKGROUND

PART ONE

INTRODUCTION

STUDYING NOVELS

Reading novels and exploring them critically can be approached in a number of ways, but when reading the text for the first time it is a good idea to consider some, or all, of the following:

- **Format and style**: how do novels differ from other genres? How are chapters or other divisions used to reveal information? Is there a narrator, and if so, how does he or she convey both his or her emotions and those of the characters?

- **The writer's perspective**: consider what the writer has to say, how he or she presents a particular view of people, the world, society, ideas, issues, etc. Are, or were, these views controversial?

- **Shape and structure**: explore how the narrative of the story develops – the moments of revelation and reflection, openings and endings, conflicts and resolutions. Is there one main plot or are there multiple plots and sub-plots?

- **Setting**: where and when is the novel set? How do the locations shape or reflect the lives and relationships of the characters?

- **Choice of language**: does the writer choose to write formally or informally? Does he or she use different registers for characters and narrators, and employ language features such as imagery and dialect?

- **Links and connections**: what other texts does this novel remind you of? Can you see connections between its narrative, characters and ideas and those of other texts you have studied? Is the novel part of a literary movement or tradition?

- **Your perspective and that of others**: what are your feelings about the novel? Can you relate to the narrators, characters, themes and ideas? What do others say about it – for example, critics or other writers?

 QUESTION

What does the setting of *Regeneration* add to the novel in terms of tone and atmosphere?

These York Notes offer an introduction to *Regeneration* and cannot substitute for close reading of the text and the study of secondary sources.

READING *REGENERATION*

Regeneration, published in 1991, was Pat Barker's fifth novel, and the first in what has become known as the '*Regeneration* trilogy'. On completing *Regeneration*, Barker continued the story of some of its characters in *The Eye in the Door* (1993) and *The Ghost Road* (1995), and they remain the works for which she is probably best known. *Regeneration* was adapted for the cinema in 1997, bringing Barker's story to an audience who might not have read her writing, and increasing interest in the novel and its sequels.

Previously, Barker had a reputation for being an author who was primarily concerned with writing about women's lives and experiences, and it was not until the publication of the novel that came before *Regeneration*, *The Man Who Wasn't There* (1988), that she began to use men as her principal characters. She has continued to do so in the novels that follow the trilogy: *Another World* (1998), *Border Crossing* (2001), *Double Vision* (2003) and *Life Class* (2007). Barker has claimed that this shift was a conscious decision because she was tired of being regarded as an author who could only write about women. In an interview, she said that 'if, as I did you write about women, sooner or later some idiot critic says: But ah, can she do men? – as if that were some kind of Everest' (Candice Robb, 'A Stomach for War', *Independent on Sunday*, 12 September 1993).

Regeneration can be classified as a historical novel, in that it attempts to realistically depict life in 1917, when the First World War was still at its height. Not only is it full of period detail, but it also features fictional versions of real people: the psychiatrists W. H. R. Rivers and Lewis Yealland, the scientist Henry Head and the war poets Siegfried Sassoon, Wilfred Owen and Robert Graves are all historical figures, and many scenes in the novel are based upon actual incidents recorded by them in memoirs and letters. However, it can be difficult to disentangle fact from fiction in this book: *Regeneration* also includes straightforwardly invented characters – such as the working-class officer Billy Prior and the munitions worker Sarah Lumb – as well as figures who could be described as 'historical extrapolations' – mainly fictional, but with a

CONTEXT

The building where the main action of *Regeneration* is set, Craiglockhart Military Hospital near Edinburgh, is now part of Napier University's Craiglockhart Campus. It is home to a permanent War Poets exhibition, which includes original documents, photographs and memorabilia from the First World War.

basis in fact. These include Rivers's patient David Burns, and Yealland's patient Callan, both of whom appear as anonymous studies in these doctors' published case-notes.

Barker's choice of a First World War setting in *Regeneration* allows her to pursue her interest, not just in men, but in masculinity – how the condition of 'being a man' is socially and culturally understood. A central **paradox** is stressed throughout the novel – that war is meant to be the most manly of activities, but the particular conditions in which the First World War was fought, particularly in the trench system of the Western Front in Belgium and France, made soldiers more like women and less like men. For Barker, this becomes crystallised in the image of the shell-shocked soldier, who becomes so mentally traumatised by enduring months, or even years, of fear and horror, that he breaks down and is unable to continue to fight. Until the First World War, hysteria was believed to be a female complaint, so when men began to suffer from it their behaviour could only be seen as 'feminine'. By placing the action in a hospital set up for the treatment of shell-shocked officers, Barker is bringing the theme of masculine crisis to the forefront of her text.

Consequently, the novel features male characters who feel themselves to be, one way or another, not 'proper' men, a concern which is most often expressed through themes of sexual inadequacy or deviation. Several of the main characters – Siegfried Sassoon, Wilfred Owen and Robert Graves – are homosexual, while Rivers is celibate and rather sexless (although there are strong suggestions that he may also be attracted to men rather than women). Only Billy Prior appears to have an active sex life with a female partner; although, weakened by chronic asthma and plagued by nightmares, he still believes that he has somehow failed as a man.

Yet the novel can also be read in a more positive way, as a text that tells a story often left out of official accounts of the First World War. Although it is male characters and experiences that dominate *Regeneration*, Barker's inclusion of the character of Sarah Lumb allows her to depict a female experience of the war. Sarah is a volunteer at a munitions factory, and she and her friends are shown to be taking full advantage of the money and independence their

CHECK THE BOOK
The madwoman is a recurring figure in nineteenth-century gothic and sensation fiction, which reinforces the association between femininity and hysteria. The most well-known example of this is the character of Bertha Mason in Charlotte Brontë's novel *Jane Eyre* (1847).

CHECK THE POEM
An indication of the admiration Sassoon felt for Rivers can be found in a poem he wrote after Rivers's death in 1922 entitled 'Revisitation'. In it, he refers to Rivers as his 'fathering friend and scientist of good', whose 'ghost … I am powerless to repay'.

CONTEXT

CONTEXT

Approximately 200,000 women were working outside the home before 1914 – by 1918, 5 million women were in employment.

war work is bringing them. Perhaps shockingly, such women do not entirely regret the conflict, but see it as a time of opportunity and freedom. In this way, Barker forces us to see that our view of the First World War has been mainly influenced by what men have written in history books and memoirs, and by the poetry of soldiers such as Owen and Sassoon. Although these accounts are important (after all, Barker refers to many of them herself in her writing of *Regeneration*), they do not tell the whole story.

What *Regeneration* is concerned with showing, therefore, is that the First World War was an event which changed everybody's lives, whether they were male or female, working or upper class, educated or not. But it didn't affect them all the same way, nor was its impact completely negative. Although the central theme of shell-shock reminds the novel's readers that it was a conflict that caused the death of hundreds of thousands of young men, and ruined the lives of thousands more, it also contributed towards the social liberation of women, and inspired many significant literary works.

Indeed, *Regeneration* can be said to be situating itself very explicitly within a pre-existing tradition of war literature. The scenes between Owen and Sassoon depict that very tradition in the process of development, as Sassoon nurtures Owen's poetic talent and edits some of his early war poems; furthermore, Barker explicitly draws upon some of the most important memoirs of the First World War, such as Sassoon's *Sherston's Progress* (1936) and Graves's *Goodbye to All That* (1929), in the writing of her own book.

CONTEXT

In her essay 'Effeminacy, Ethnicity and the End of Trauma: The Sufferings of Shell-Shocked men in Great Britain and Ireland 1914–1939' (*Journal of Contemporary History* 35:1, 2000), the historian Joanna Bourke claims that in the 1920s over 6,000 men remained hospitalised due to war trauma.

An important question that can be asked of *Regeneration* is: can it be called a 'war novel'? After all, it is not set on the battlefields, nor does it contain any detailed depictions of warfare. This is because Barker's main interest is in the effects of war upon the minds of those who experience it. Although none of the action actually takes place on the front line where the First World War was being fought, Barker constantly superimposes the landscape of conflict upon the scenery of the home front, through both the recollections of the traumatised soldiers whom Rivers is treating, and her references to the war poetry of Owen and Sassoon. In this way, our definition of war as a definable, finite event is challenged, since *Regeneration*'s portrayal of trauma forces us to think of war as something that does not come to a close at the end of a battle. Those soldiers who return from the front may have physically left the battlefield, but their amnesia, nightmares, stammering and paralysis dramatically indicate that they cannot leave the war behind as easily as that.

Regeneration itself also demonstrates the inescapability of the Great War as a subject for fiction, and can be situated alongside a general revival of interest in the First World War that began in the latter half of the twentieth century. The fiftieth anniversary of the war fell between 1964 and 1968, and this inspired a growing realisation that the numbers of survivors of the conflict were dwindling fast. Classic literary works by such writers as Sassoon, Graves and Blunden (who were all still alive) were reissued, the BBC screened *The Great War*, a documentary series which used archive footage of the battlefields, and war poetry began to be studied as part of the school curriculum. It was in the sixties, too, that the dominant myth of the Great War – as an essentially senseless event which was **tragically** wasteful of human life – began to be widely disseminated. This can be traced to the powerful pacifist sentiments being expressed in society at large: the Cuban Missile Crisis of 1962, in which the world seemed, for a tense few days, on the brink of all-out nuclear war, plus the ongoing conflict in Vietnam, inspired widespread antiwar protests in Britain, America and elsewhere.

In his work *The Great War: Myth and Memory* (2005) the historian Dan Todman notes that 'Perhaps surprisingly, there was no great wave of new prose writing to meet the upsurge in the interest in the First World War in the 1960s' (p. 157). Although a few significant novels appeared in the seventies and eighties, including Susan Hill's *Strange Meeting* (1971) and *How Many Miles to Babylon?* by Jennifer Johnston (1974), the bulk of contemporary fiction taking the First World War as its subject began to appear in the 1990s. Novels such as Mark Helprin's *A Soldier of the Great War* (1991), *Birdsong* by Sebastian Faulks (1993), *Brother to Dragons* by David Hartnett (1998), Adam Thorpe's *Nineteen Twenty-One* (2001) and Ben Elton's *The First Casualty* (2005) are similarly concerned with exploring the experience of the war from a modern perspective. *Regeneration* is a major, and very influential, contribution to this trend.

CONTEXT

In the actor Victor Spinetti's Afterword to the Methuen edition of the **satire** *Oh! What a Lovely War*, which was based around performances of original popular songs of the First World War, he describes his initial reservations about appearing in the play in 1963: 'I didn't relish the idea of a show about World War One. The thought of that war made me sick. Poppy Day, the Last Post, silence at the Cenotaph! All those young lives lost! To what purpose?'

CHECK THE BOOK

Barker explores this idea in greater detail in a later novel, *Another World*, published in 1998. Although it is set in the present, it features a hundred-year-old survivor of the First World War, Geordie, who remains haunted by his memories of the conflict and frequently returns to the battlefield in his mind. As his grandson observes, 'Geordie's past isn't over. It isn't even the past'.

The reader of *Regeneration* will be presented with different stories about the First World War, and reminded of the suffering of those who survived. Written in a period in which there was a growing awareness that direct experience of the First World War was slipping away from living memory, *Regeneration*, like other contemporary Great War novels, can be regarded as a literary memorial to one of the most devastating conflicts in history. As Barker herself says, it is 'about a period of the world's history that we have never come to terms with. The Somme is like the Holocaust. It revealed things about mankind that we cannot come to terms with and cannot forget. It never becomes the past' (Candice Rodd, 'A Stomach for War', *Independent on Sunday*, 12 September 1993).

Part Two

The Text

Note on the Text

Regeneration was first published in 1991 by Viking. The edition used in these Notes is the Penguin paperback edition, published in 1992.

In 1996, after Pat Barker won the Booker Prize for *The Ghost Road*, Viking republished a single-volume edition of all three novels in the series – *Regeneration, The Eye in the Door* and *The Ghost Road* – under the title *The Regeneration Trilogy*. Penguin published it in paperback in 1998, but it is now out of print.

CONTEXT

The Booker Prize is a prestigious literary award given annually to a full-length novel written by a citizen of the Commonwealth or the Republic of Ireland, and published in English.

Synopsis

Regeneration is set during the First World War in 1917. When it begins, the psychiatrist W. H. R. Rivers is awaiting the arrival of Siegfried Sassoon at Craiglockhart Hospital. Sassoon, a distinguished officer, has been referred there by a Medical Board following his refusal to fight. He has published his objections in an article entitled 'Finished with the War: *A Soldier's Declaration*', which Rivers has read. Sassoon is reluctant to go to hospital, understanding that if he is diagnosed as suffering from war trauma, or shell-shock, it can be used by the authorities to explain away his protest as the product of an unbalanced mind. Rivers's job is to determine whether Sassoon is traumatised or fully in control of his thoughts and actions, and to persuade him to return to active military service.

CONTEXT

Dr W. H. R. Rivers (1864–1922) was a psychiatrist and anthropologist, who treated shell-shock patients at Craiglockhart Military Hospital between 1916 and 1917.

Much of the novel is concerned with the interviews that take place between Sassoon and Rivers, during which Rivers decides that Sassoon is not suffering from war trauma. His tactic is to challenge Sassoon's sense of honour: known to be a conscientious officer and devoted to his men, Sassoon will, Rivers thinks, eventually decide that it is his duty to return to war. However, in the course of their

CONTEXT

Siegfried Sassoon (1886–1967) is now regarded as one of Britain's most famous war poets. He enlisted in the Royal Welch Fusiliers and served with distinction, being awarded the Military Cross in 1916.

debates, Rivers begins to find that his own views concerning the war are beginning to change. He begins the novel convinced that it must be fought to the bitter end, but becomes increasingly concerned about his role in 'curing' young men of their psychological symptoms, only to send them back to the conditions that caused them to break down in the first place. He begins to see all symptoms of war trauma – stammering, nightmares, amnesia and paralysis – as an antiwar protest that is every bit as eloquent as Sassoon's.

Rivers's growing uncertainty concerning the war and his part in it is magnified by his encounters with other patients. At the time of Sassoon's admission to Craiglockhart, he is struggling with a seemingly incurable case, that of a young officer called David Burns, who cannot eat after having been blown up and landing head-first in a decomposing body. Soon afterwards, he admits a new patient, Billy Prior, who is dumb and suffering from amnesia. Prior soon recovers his voice, but proves to be extremely difficult to deal with. He is unusual because, unlike the majority of the officers in the hospital, he is working class. He is hostile to Rivers's methods, and often refuses to answer his questions. Instead, he keeps asking personal questions of Rivers himself, refusing to allow him to remain detached and analytical. Prior claims that Rivers is as traumatised as any of the men he treats, putting forward as evidence the fact that Rivers himself has a stammer – a speech defect he has had since childhood.

CHECK THE POEM

The material benefits of being a munitions worker are described in Madeline Ida Bedford's poem 'Munition Wages', in which a munitions worker celebrates the fact that the money she earns buys her 'bracelets and jewellery, / Rings envied by friends; / A Sergeant to swank with, / And something to lend'.

On a night out in Edinburgh, Prior meets Sarah Lumb, a girl from Newcastle who has come to the city to work in a munitions factory. She and her friends are enjoying the freedom of being away from home and the money that they are earning, which is far more than anything they could expect in peacetime. Prior begins a relationship with Sarah, and, on a day-trip to the coast, they become lovers. Sarah's mother does not approve of her work or her choice of boyfriend, arguing that she is putting herself at risk of an unwanted pregnancy, and should save herself for marriage. Sarah disagrees, and she and Prior become increasingly close. Near the end of the novel he sneaks into her lodgings where, as they begin to undress each other, he tells her that he loves her.

In order to cure Prior of his amnesia, Rivers hypnotises him. Prior recalls an incident in which two members of his platoon were blown to bits by a shell, and he had to gather up the pieces from the floor of the trench. His breakdown occurred when he picked up an intact eyeball and looked at it lying in the palm of his hand. Prior is angry that an event that seems to him so relatively trivial could have caused his breakdown. He thinks it indicates that he is weak, although Rivers assures him that symptoms are often the product of stress suffered over a period of time, and that under such conditions, anyone could break down. Prior's hope of returning to the front is compromised, however, by the discovery that he suffers from severe asthma.

Under the pressure of constant work, little rest and his growing doubts about his work, Rivers eventually breaks down himself and has to take a holiday away from the hospital. He spends part of his leave at his brother's chicken farm, and this inspires him to reminisce about his childhood and his authoritarian father, a speech therapist, who attempted – unsuccessfully – to cure his son's stammer. Rivers then goes to visit his old friend and scientific collaborator Henry Head in London. Head offers him a job working with traumatised pilots in the Royal Flying Corps which Rivers is tempted by, but reluctant to accept.

Before he returns to Craiglockhart, Rivers visits Burns – who has been invalided out of the army – at his home in Aldeburgh in Suffolk. While he is there, Burns has a traumatic episode when he leaves the house during a storm in the middle of the night. Rivers finds him standing staring up at a tower by the sea, and experiences a moment of intense anger at witnessing Burns's continuing suffering. Before the war he was a young man full of promise, and the horrors he has endured on the battlefield have taken that away from him. Although he seems to have recovered somewhat, Rivers cannot believe that Burns will ever be the same person he once was.

During his stay at the hospital, Sassoon meets another patient, Wilfred Owen, who is an aspiring poet. Owen hero-worships Sassoon, an already successful poet, and Sassoon begins to help him

CONTEXT

Wilfred Owen (1893–1918) served with the Manchester Regiment. He died, aged twenty-five, on the Sambre-Oise Canal in France a week before the signing of the Armistice that brought the war to an end. He is now regarded as one of Britain's most important poets of the First World War.

write his own poems about the war. He also publishes some of his own poetry in the hospital magazine that Owen edits, called the *Hydra*.

In spite of this activity, Sassoon misses Rivers during his absence, realising that he has come to regard him as a father-figure. When Rivers returns, Sassoon tells him that he has decided to give up his protest and return to active service. Rivers says that he is pleased, but he continues to experience doubts about the role he has played in bringing Sassoon to this decision. However, he also feels a certain sense of relief. During their therapy sessions, Rivers has become aware that Sassoon is homosexual, the practice of which is illegal. One MP in particular, Pemberton Billing, has vowed to make public the names of prominent homosexuals in Britain, and Rivers believes that, if he were to continue his protest, Sassoon himself could become a target of this campaign.

> **CONTEXT**
>
> Homosexuality remained illegal in England and Wales until 1967. It was not legalised in Scotland until 1980.

At the next Medical Board, it is decided that Prior is fit for home service only – a ruling that Prior resents bitterly. However, when he says goodbye to Rivers, he finally manages to mutter an ungracious, but genuine, expression of gratitude. Sassoon gets impatient waiting for his turn because it is making him late for a social engagement, so he leaves early. Rivers is furious, as this means Sassoon will have to remain in the hospital until another Board can be convened. Owen is returning to active service, and he and Sassoon have a final dinner together, during which the real nature of the affection between the two men remains unspoken. When Sassoon leaves, Owen feels an enormous sense of loss.

Rivers decides to accept the job in London, and moves there before Sassoon goes before his second Medical Board. He has been invited to witness the work of a fellow psychiatrist, Dr Lewis Yealland, but is disturbed by what he sees. Yealland cures a dumb soldier by locking him into the treatment room and repeatedly applying strong electrical currents to his throat. The method works, and the soldier is able to speak again after only a single session. After visiting Yealland, Rivers has a nightmare in which he is forcing a horse's bit into a soldier's mouth. He interprets the dream as meaning that he and Yealland are not so very different after all, in spite of their very different methods. Like Yealland, Rivers is silencing antiwar protest – Sassoon's in particular.

Henry Head reassures Rivers that this is not what the dream means at all, and Rivers in turn acknowledges the positive aspects of his changing opinions. He returns to Craiglockhart for Sassoon's Medical Board, where the latter is pronounced to be fit to return to the front. However, he still refuses to recant his protest, although he argues that it is nevertheless his duty to go back. Rivers worries that the contradictions in this position will cause Sassoon to break down again, or even actively pursue his own death. But he can do nothing more than to officially record that Sassoon has been discharged from the hospital as fit for active duty.

Regeneration's central focus on the association between W. H. R. Rivers and Sassoon is indicated in the way in which the **narrative** is divided up into four sections, each of which ends with a significant development in their relationship. The first, from Chapter 1 to 7, opens with Rivers's uncertainty regarding Sassoon's case, as he awaits the latter's arrival at Craiglockhart, and ends with his decision that Sassoon is not suffering from war neurosis. The second, covering Chapters 8–13, ends with Rivers's departure from Craiglockhart on leave, and Sassoon's realisation that he regards Rivers as a second father. Sassoon is largely absent from the third section, from Chapters 14 to 16, which follows Rivers's experiences while he is away from the hospital, but it concludes with Sassoon disclosing to Rivers his decision to return to active duty. The final section (Chapters 17–23) covers Sassoon's final Medical Board and Rivers signing the papers that formally discharge him from the hospital. Although stories involving other characters – some completely separate from both Rivers and Sassoon – are woven through all four sections, they tend to amplify the main plot-line in the ways in which they either contrast with or echo it.

CONTEXT

Dr Lewis Yealland was a neurologist based at the National Hospital for the Paralysed and Epileptic in London, and was known for his use of electric-shock treatment on shell-shock patients.

DETAILED SUMMARIES

CHAPTER 1

- W. H. R. Rivers reads Siegfried Sassoon's *A Soldier's Declaration*.
- Sassoon makes the journey from Liverpool to Edinburgh.
- In a flashback we learn how Robert Graves persuaded Sassoon to attend the Medical Board that sends him to Craiglockhart Military Hospital.
- Rivers sees Sassoon arrive.

The novel opens with the psychiatrist W. H. R. Rivers awaiting the arrival of the war poet Siegfried Sassoon at Craiglockhart Military Hospital near Edinburgh. He reads out Sassoon's Declaration, dated July 1917, in which the poet states his opposition to the continuation of the First World War, and discusses Sassoon's case with Major William Bryce, Commandant of Craiglockhart. Sassoon is being sent to the hospital to be treated for shell-shock, but Rivers is not entirely convinced that this is the right course of action. He is concerned that the diagnosis is rather convenient, given that the alternative is a prison term for refusing to return to fight at the front, and worries that Sassoon's presence at Craiglockhart might reflect badly on the hospital, which could be accused of sheltering cowards and 'conchies' (p. 4).

CONTEXT

'Conchies' is dismissive shorthand for 'conscientious objectors', who refused to fight on moral or religious grounds. After the British government passed the first of several conscription laws in 1916, it became illegal for men to refuse to join the army if judged fit to do so. Those who continued to resist were imprisoned.

The perspective then moves to Sassoon, who is catching a train from Liverpool to Edinburgh. He is expecting to meet his friend, Robert Graves, at the station at Liverpool, but he doesn't turn up and Sassoon has to make his journey alone. In a series of **flashbacks**, it is disclosed that it was Graves who arranged for Sassoon to appear before the Medical Board that sent him to Craiglockhart. Although Sassoon argues that his protest is necessary, and that he wants to be publicly court-martialled in order to state his objection to the war, Graves is not only concerned this will never be allowed to happen, but also that Sassoon is genuinely traumatised, even if he won't admit it.

We then return to Craiglockhart, where Rivers, still pondering Sassoon's case, sees the latter's taxi arriving. Unaware that he is being observed, Sassoon hesitates before entering the hospital, and Rivers feels ashamed that he has witnessed a private moment of fear.

COMMENTARY

Although this chapter is short, it introduces one of the novel's most important, and complicated, dilemmas: is Sassoon's protest against the war a rational one, or is it a symptom of war trauma? His Declaration, which is reproduced in full at the very beginning of the novel, is lucidly written and conveys a convincing argument, but considering that it was written at the height of the First World War it is alarmingly radical. Rivers **ironically** draws attention to another problematic aspect of Sassoon's protest when he observes that the signature at the bottom of the Declaration, 'S. Sassoon', omits his first name, and that this might be thought significant: 'The "S" stands for "Siegfried". Apparently he thought that was better left out' (p. 3).

'Siegfried' is a German name, and could suggest that the writer has been inspired to call for an end to the war out of sympathy for the enemy. (We only learn later in the book that Siegfried Sassoon was given his first name by a father who loved the work of the composer Wagner.) Rivers's subsequent conversation with Bryce sets out the stark choice faced by Sassoon – prison or psychiatric hospital – and this is reiterated in the section of the chapter **narrated** from Sassoon's **point of view**, in which Graves argues strongly that Sassoon cannot become the kind of 'martyr' (p. 6) he aspires to be. His intention to force a court-martial in order to initiate a public debate on the validity of continuing the war is unrealistic, since the authorities will ensure that he is silenced, one way or the other.

Although Sassoon denies that he is suffering from shell-shock, or neurasthenia, Barker gives her readers cause to doubt this. During the train journey to Craiglockhart, he recollects that the unexpected appearance of Graves in the lounge of the Exchange Hotel in Liverpool makes him briefly think that he is 'hallucinating again' (p. 5). Hallucinations are a common shell-shock symptom, and it seems that Sassoon is accustomed to seeing things that aren't

CONTEXT

'Shell-shock' is the **colloquial** term for war trauma, and was coined in 1915 by the psychiatrist Dr Charles Myers. A more precise medical term was 'neurasthenia', which describes a psychological disorder characterised by depression, irritability and fatigue. It came into circulation in 1869, but was used in the First World War to describe the symptoms of war trauma characteristically experienced by the officer class.

CONTEXT

Robert Graves (1895–1985) was a poet, novelist and translator, who served in the Royal Welch Fusiliers during the First World War. He wrote about his friendship with Sassoon in his memoir *Goodbye to All That* (1929).

CHECK THE POEM

Sassoon's **allusion** to 'lines of men with grey muttering faces' echoes his poem 'Attack', which was published in *Counter-Attack and Other Poems* (1918): 'Men jostle and climb to meet the bristling fire. / Lines of grey muttering faces, masked with fear'.

actually there. Later, Graves reveals that Sassoon has written him a letter in which he describes seeing corpses lying in the streets of Piccadilly, and although readers do not witness Sassoon experiencing this horrific vision first hand, the sound of the conductor's whistle on the station platform momentarily catapults him back to the front line, where he sees 'lines of men with grey muttering faces clambering up the ladders to face the guns' (p. 5).

The first chapter introduces us to two of the main characters in the novel who are based on actual historical figures, Siegfried Sassoon and Dr W. H. R. Rivers. In fact, the other two **protagonists** that also appear in this chapter, Robert Graves and William Bryce, as well as others mentioned in passing but who are not seen, also really existed, indicating the extent to which *Regeneration* is based on historical source material.

GLOSSARY	
4	**scrimshankers** military slang for skivers, people who avoid work
4	**Lees-Smith** H. B. Lees-Smith, Liberal MP for Northampton
6	**Russell** Bertrand Russell (1872–1970), a philosopher and thinker who was active in the pacifist movement during the First World War
7	**court-martial** military court
7	**Piccadilly** street in London W1
8	**MC** Military Cross. Instituted in 1914, the Military Cross is given to officers of the British Army as an award for bravery on active service
8	**MO** Medical Officer

CHAPTER 2

- Sassoon and Rivers have their first meeting.
- Sassoon maintains his antiwar stance, claiming that he no longer dislikes the Germans, but hates British civilians, who support the war but do not fight themselves.
- Rivers tells Sassoon that it is his job to change Sassoon's mind.
- Rivers feels defeated by the case of Burns, who cannot eat after involuntarily ingesting human flesh in a battlefield incident.

Sassoon has his first interview with Rivers. Sassoon tells Rivers about the Medical Board, as well as some of his battlefield experiences in which he deliberately placed himself in danger. He is concerned with proving to Rivers that he is not suffering from a war neurosis: when Rivers observes that 'taking *unnecessary* risks is one of the first signs of a war neurosis' (p. 12), he retorts that he was frequently ordered to do unnecessarily risky things by his superior officers. He believes that he has written some good poems while in hospital, and that he couldn't have done so in a traumatised state – although he does admit to having suffered from hallucinations and nightmares. Rivers, however, reassures him that such symptoms do not necessarily mean that he is going mad. Sassoon also begins to tell Rivers things that he didn't tell the Medical Board, confessing that he no longer dislikes the Germans as much as British civilians, who support the war unthinkingly and have no knowledge of the real suffering endured by the soldiers on the front line.

Rivers sees Sassoon picking at the loose thread on the front of his jacket where his Military Cross was once sewn, and Sassoon describes how he felt when he threw it into the Mersey as a protest against the war. He acknowledges that it was a futile gesture, but maintains that it was still a necessary one. Rivers jokes that Sassoon is not suffering from a war neurosis, but an antiwar neurosis, and reminds him that it is 'my duty to … to try and change that' (p. 15).

CONTEXT

This conversation is taken from Sassoon's memoir *Sherston's Progress* (1936), in which he describes his first appointment with Rivers: 'One evening I asked whether he thought I was suffering from shell-shock. "Certainly not," he replied. "What *have* I got, then?" "Well, you appear to be suffering from an anti-war complex." We both of us laughed at that' (p. 518).

At dinner that evening, Rivers tells Bryce that he cannot find
anything wrong with Sassoon, and that he finds him a likeable
individual. Sassoon's conversation about golf with another inmate is
interrupted by a young man, Burns, who begins vomiting
uncontrollably. Burns is taken out of the dining room by two
nurses, and Rivers follows. We learn that Burns cannot eat
following an experience in which he was blown up and landed face-
down in a rotting German corpse, his nose and mouth filling with
decomposing flesh. Rivers goes to his own room tormented by the
knowledge that he does not know how help Burns accept the horror
of what has happened to him. He looks out of his window to see
Graves finally arriving at the hospital.

COMMENTARY

The main **point of view** in this chapter is that of Rivers. In the first
section, he is beginning his preliminary assessment of Sassoon's
condition. The closeness with which he is studying his new patient
is shown in the amount of **narrative** description of Sassoon's
actions, speech, appearance and reactions. In contrast, there is very
little description of Rivers himself, indicating that his role is to keep
in the background and encourage Sassoon to voice his feelings and
experiences. Quite frequently Rivers does not say anything when
Sassoon stops talking, so their exchange is punctuated by pauses and
prolonged silences, which Rivers only interrupts to prompt Sassoon
to carry on speaking. Although the conversation appears quite
friendly – supported later in the chapter, when Rivers admits to
Bryce that he likes Sassoon 'very much' (p. 16) – it reflects the
relationship between patient and doctor that Rivers is seeking to
establish. Rivers reminds Sassoon of this at the end of their meeting,
when he warns him that, as a doctor in the British Army, he 'can't
pretend to be neutral' (p. 15). The mention of Sassoon's meaningful
glance at 'both their uniforms' (p. 15) further reminds the reader
that Rivers is part of the very military machine against which
Sassoon is protesting.

The second part of the chapter immerses itself in Sassoon's point of
view only briefly before returning to Rivers and his inability to cure
Burns of his traumatically induced eating disorder. Burns is one of
several characters in the novel who are fictionalised representations

of actual soldiers treated at Craiglockhart. In *Regeneration*, he becomes **symbolic** of the human cost of the First World War. While his wounds may not be physical, he is nevertheless a casualty of war who will never be able to live a normal life again. Although he is used to dealing with patients who have endured horrific experiences, Rivers has an intense feeling of helplessness in relation to Burns's case because he can 'find no redeeming feature' (p. 19) that will enable Burns to accept what has happened to him.

There is a clear contrast between Rivers's attitude in the first and second sections of the chapter. With Sassoon, he is detached, analytical and conscious of the purpose of his job, which is to make men fit to return to battle. But with Burns, the reader not only begins to see his more compassionate side, but also the confusion that Rivers conceals beneath his professional façade. As a doctor working for the military, he should support the war: but when faced with the wasted body and ruined life of Burns, he cannot truly believe that the horror involved in warfare can ever be justified. This is the introduction of a dilemma that will intensify as the narrative progresses.

CONTEXT

The character of David Burns is drawn from an anonymous case-study described by Rivers in a paper he delivered to the Royal Society of Medicine in December 1917, entitled 'The Repression of War Experience'. Rivers is depicted writing this paper in Chapters 15 and 22 of *Regeneration*.

GLOSSARY

12	**battalion HQ** the headquarters of a military unit within a regiment, situated behind the front line
13	**pacifist** someone who is opposed to war and campaigns to bring it to an end
13	**second-lieutenant** lowest officer rank in the British army
14	**attrition** the act of wearing an opponent down through constant attack
14	**civilians** those who are not serving members of the armed forces
14	**certify** to formally determine that an individual is in need of psychiatric treatment
15	**Mersey** river running through Liverpool
15	**acquiesce** give in, submit
16	**cadets** those being trained to be army officers

continued

16	trench mortar bombs bombs fired from a trench mortar – a short tube that shot the bomb out over the top of the trench at a steep angle
17	RAMC Royal Army Medical Corps
17	Bedlam Popular term for lunatic asylum originating from the Bethlem Royal Hospital in London, established in the fourteenth century
17	VADs Women's Voluntary Aid Detachment. See **Historical background: Women's war work**
17	trench a deep ditch in which soldiers sheltered out of sight of the enemy, and a particular feature of the French and Belgian battlefields
19	alimentary canal the passage food follows through the body, from mouth to large intestine

CHAPTER 3

- Graves arrives at Craiglockhart, and has a meeting with Rivers.
- Graves tells Rivers how he convinced the Medical Board that Sassoon's protest was caused by illness rather than a rational desire to bring the war to an end.
- Rivers reads Sassoon's poetry for the first time, and decides it illustrates the complexity of his case.

Sassoon meets Graves outside Craiglockhart, and takes him to see Rivers. Rivers is particularly interested in hearing more about the Medical Board that sent Sassoon to the hospital, and Graves explains why he arranged it. He is of the opinion that Sassoon's protest was a hopeless cause that would achieve nothing apart from ending Sassoon's military career in disgrace. He says that Sassoon is 'the best platoon commander I've ever known' (p. 21), who is as devoted to his men as they are to him, and that he has to be able to return to them in the future if he wishes to do so.

CONTEXT

Pacifists faced a difficult situation in the First World War. Men who refused to join up for conscientious reasons could be allowed to work in non-combat roles, such as hospital orderlies or stretcher-bearers, but after the introduction of compulsory conscription they faced the possibility of imprisonment and considerable hardship and persecution.

Graves goes on to admit that he lied, both to Sassoon and to the Board, in order to achieve this, convincing Sassoon that he would never achieve his goal of being publicly court-martialled, and refraining from telling the officers on the Board everything that Sassoon had threatened to do, such as assassinate the Prime Minister. Graves confesses that he actually sympathises with Sassoon's opinions about the war, but thinks Sassoon is taking the wrong course of action in writing his Declaration. He believes that Sassoon was misled by pacifists such as Bertrand Russell, to whom Graves has now written in order to demand that he has no further contact with Sassoon.

After Graves has left, Rivers opens an envelope that Graves has given him, which contains three war poems Sassoon wrote in hospital. Rivers decides that they reveal that Sassoon is dealing with war trauma in the opposite way to most of his patients. Whereas soldiers tend to want to forget the war, which means that their memories resurface in the form of nightmares, Sassoon seems to be doing everything he can to keep remembering it. This, reflects Rivers, might explain why he is no longer suffering from bad dreams and hallucinations, but could make persuading him to return to active service 'a much more complicated and risky business than he had thought' (p. 26).

COMMENTARY

The encounter between Graves and Rivers is important in adding further details to what the reader has learnt in the first two chapters of the novel regarding Sassoon's antiwar protest and Graves's role in arranging the Medical Board that sends him to Craiglockhart. Sassoon's **point of view** regarding these events was portrayed in the first chapter, but now we see it from Graves's perspective. His account stresses the seriousness of Sassoon's condition at the time he wrote the Declaration: his claim that Sassoon was at one time threatening 'to kill Lloyd George' (p. 22) suggests the ravings of a man on the verge of insanity. Yet at the same time, Graves presents Sassoon's protest as a rational one, claiming that he is 'talking sense about the war' (p. 23).

> **CONTEXT**
>
> Lady Ottoline Morrell (1873–1938) (p. 23) was a notable society hostess who also influenced Sassoon's growing interest in the antiwar movement. Along with her husband, the Liberal MP Philip Morrell, and the philosopher Bertrand Russell, she was a leading pacifist during the First World War. Sassoon met her during his time in hospital in Oxford in August 1916, and she invited him to her country house, Garsington Manor, to complete his convalescence.

CONTEXT

The First World
War in the Middle
East was fought in
Syria, Sinai and
Palestine. British
forces were sent
there in 1915 to
defend the Suez
Canal, a vital link
between Europe
and Asia, from
attacks by the
Ottoman (Turkish)
Empire, an ally of
Germany. Graves
hoped to be
posted there
following his
convalescence, but
as his health did
not recover
enough for him to
return to active
service he never
achieved his goal
of being sent to
the Middle East.

Graves's description of Sassoon is therefore **paradoxical**, because it presents him as both mad and sane. He knows that Sassoon was suffering from hallucinations and nightmares when he wrote the Declaration, but does not disagree with the ideas expressed within it. In fact, his desire to have Sassoon sent to hospital does not seem to originate from a belief that he needs to be treated for a mental disorder so much as a personal concern to save a friend from the consequences of his actions. He thinks Sassoon is a courageous soldier and a much-respected officer who should not be permitted to end his military career in disgrace, and sees commitment to Craiglockhart as a functional way of ensuring that Sassoon can eventually return to active service.

As well as continuing the debate over whether Sassoon is or is not suffering from shell-shock, Graves's description of his role in arranging the Medical Board brings what will be an important recurring theme to the forefront of the novel. He persuades Sassoon, he tells Rivers, 'to say nothing' (p. 22) in front of the Board; and although this is done out of a belief that he is acting in his friend's best interests, the idea of silence, of not being able – or not being permitted – to speak, will become a central concern in *Regeneration*.

This chapter also demonstrates some of Barker's most obvious blending of fact with fiction. The verses that Graves gives Rivers – 'To the Warmongers', 'The General' and an early draft of 'The Rear Guard' (which is left untitled in the novel) – are not her own inventions, but are authentic poems by the real Sassoon, first published in 1918 in his first book, *Counter-Attack and Other Poems*. There is deliberate **irony** in Barker's portrayal of Rivers's reaction upon reading them: she, like her readers, knows that Siegfried Sassoon is now one of the most famous of the poets of the First World War, but in her novel she creates a scene in which his work is being seen for the first time by somebody who has no knowledge of poetry. For Rivers, these pieces are of use only to be analysed as a clue to Sassoon's state of mind. They do not, though, solve his dilemma as to how to treat his new patient, since they indicate that he has not suppressed his traumatic memories as most shell-shocked soldiers do, and stress his role as an oddity in the world of Craiglockhart.

GLOSSARY

21	**convalescent home** place where an individual is sent after being discharged from hospital in order to complete his or her process of recovery
21	**Isle of Wight** small British island situated in the Channel off the south coast of England
21	**platoon commander** the officer in charge of a platoon, a small group of around thirty soldiers. He would usually be a lower-ranked officer, such as a lieutenant
21	**CO** Commanding Officer
21	**Litherland** a suburb of Liverpool, and site of the Wartime Training Depot for the 3rd (Reserve) Battalion of the Royal Welch Fusiliers between 1915 and 1917
22	**VC** Victoria Cross, the highest military decoration awarded to soldiers for 'valour in the face of the enemy'
22	**Lloyd George** David Lloyd George (1863–1945), Prime Minister of Great Britain from 1916 to 1922
25	**Warmongers** those who encourage the pursuit of war
25	**kindles** lights or sets on fire
26	**precipitated** caused something to happen rapidly
26	**therapeutic** aiding the process of healing

CONTEXT

Arras (p. 25) was the site of two significant battles in the First World war, in 1914 and 1917. The earlier engagement, however, involved only the French army: the one Sassoon is writing about is the Battle of Arras fought between April and May, 1917. It ended in victory for the Allied forces, but at the cost of thousands of lives on both sides.

CHAPTER 4

- Rivers has a consultation with another of his patients, Captain Anderson, and they discuss his strange dreams.
- Sassoon and Graves go for a swim.
- Rivers has a second meeting with Sassoon.
- Burns runs away from Craiglockhart and conducts a strange ritual in the countryside.

The chapter begins with another of Rivers's therapy sessions, this time with Captain Anderson, a former surgeon who has broken down while working at a hospital behind the front lines in France. The main symptom of his trauma is an inability to bear the sight of blood. Anderson describes a nightmare in which he realises he is naked in front of his wife and her friends. When he runs away from them, he is chased by his father-in-law and tied up with a pair of women's corsets. He awakes, screaming and vomiting, from the nightmare's final scene, in which Rivers appears wearing a post-mortem apron and gloves. Anderson finds the dream embarrassing because of what he thinks is its sexual content, but Rivers interprets it differently, arguing that it represents Anderson's fear of returning to his surgical career. He also becomes privately concerned that it suggests Anderson may be experiencing suicidal thoughts.

The scene then shifts to the swimming pool at Craiglockhart, and a conversation between Sassoon and Graves. Graves notices the scar on Sassoon's shoulder, and Sassoon, in turn, looks at the shrapnel wound on Graves's thigh, joking that he was extremely lucky he hadn't been hit a little higher up. This causes him to recall a less fortunate case he encountered while in hospital: a boy left with nothing but 'a neat little hole … between the legs' (p. 33).

Rivers has his second consultation with Sassoon, and they begin to discuss the topic of fathers. Rivers asks Sassoon about his own father, who left the family when Sassoon was five, and died when he was eight. Sassoon says he feels that he would have achieved more in life had his father remained alive, and that 'the army's probably the only place I've ever really belonged' (p. 36). Rivers ends the interview by confronting Sassoon with the fact that if he keeps his protest up, he will ensure his personal safety while his comrades die on the battlefields.

The final section of the chapter reintroduces Burns, who decides to go on a trip outside the hospital. He leaves with no clear idea of where he's going, and ends up in the countryside outside Edinburgh. Alarmed on encountering a tree hung with the bodies of dead animals 'in various stages of decay' (p. 38), he initially flees, but, imagining Rivers advising him not to run away, returns. He takes the corpses down from the tree and arranges them in a circle with himself, naked, seated in the middle. On his return to the hospital much later, Burns finds everyone worried by his disappearance. When he wakes later in the night, he discovers Rivers

---

CONTEXT

Sassoon's father Alfred left his wife and children in 1891 – according to Sassoon's biographer Jean Moorcroft Wilson, he ran away 'with the novelist Constance Fletcher, who wrote under the pseudonym George Fleming and who had been a close friend of Oscar Wilde' (*Siegfried Sassoon: The Making of a War Poet*, 1998, p. 39). Alfred died of tuberculosis in 1895.

sitting beside his bed watching him sleep, and realises that it was because of him that he decided to come back.

COMMENTARY

The length of this chapter indicates the increasing range of Barker's **narrative** perspective, which moves between all three of the most important characters introduced to the book so far: Rivers, Sassoon and Burns. The conversation between Rivers and Anderson with which it opens is significant on a number of levels. It explicitly recalls the sessions we have already witnessed with Sassoon and Burns: for example, Anderson comments **satirically** on Rivers's habit of remaining silent in order to encourage his patient to talk further, a technique we have already seen him employ with great effect in his interview with Sassoon. The compassion that has been demonstrated in Rivers's interactions with Burns is also evident, particularly in his private worries that Anderson might be suicidal. But Anderson is a much less sympathetic figure than either Sassoon or Burns. His medical training causes him to think, at times, that he knows better than Rivers, and his retorts to Rivers's questions are often extremely defensive.

Anderson's main usefulness to the narrative is to introduce the chapter's central concern with masculine identity and male authority. His basic knowledge of the ideas of Sigmund Freud lead him to interpret his own dream as indicating a fear that because he has broken down he is no longer a 'proper' man: he is tied up in 'lady's corsets' (p. 28), and beaten with a stick which has a hissing snake – a stereotypical Freudian phallic **symbol** – coiled around it. He is surprised that Rivers does not actually think the dream represents any of these things. But the appearance of Rivers in the conclusion of Anderson's dream, whatever it might signify, does indicate Rivers's importance in the minds of his patients, which is a heavy responsibility for one man to bear.

Although Rivers dismisses Anderson's concerns regarding his sexuality, it is this **motif** that is expanded upon in the subsequent scene between Graves and Sassoon, which is preoccupied with the idea of castration, or the loss of male genitalia. This, it seems, is the central **paradox** of war. Although being a soldier is traditionally an

> **CONTEXT**
>
> The word 'caduceus' (p. 29) refers to a staff entwined with two snakes and topped with a pair of wings: the traditional symbol for medicine and healing. The Royal Army Medical Corps, of which Anderson and Rivers are members, uses as its emblem a staff with a snake coiled around it. The snake is also a symbol of regeneration, due to its ability to rejuvenate itself by shedding its skin.

> **CONTEXT**
>
> Sigmund Freud (1856–1939) was the founder of the science of psychoanalysis, or the study of the unconscious workings of the human mind. Works such as *The Interpretation of Dreams* (1899) were influential in the early treatment of shell-shock.

extremely manly pursuit, it can deprive a man of his masculinity: either literally, as in Sassoon's recollections of the boy in the hospital, or symbolically, causing surgeons to collapse at the sight of blood, and courageous fighters to become weeping, trembling hysterics.

The rather strange incident involving Burns concludes this contemplation of masculinity and castration. Whereas Anderson's dream is interpreted for the reader – even if no definite understanding of it is reached – Burns's experience is related with no attempt at explanation. The narrative is, for the moment, located in Burns's own mind, and he does not understand what compels him to engage in such a strange ritual. But if the reader has paid attention to the issues debated by the other characters in the chapter, an interpretation of this event is possible. Obvious parallels exist between the muddy field containing animal corpses and the battlefields of France, which suggests that Burns is trying to achieve some kind of reconciliation with his memories by symbolically returning to the scene of his trauma. The linking of shell-shock with masculinity is hinted at in Burns's contemplation of his own genitals, which he sees as 'incongruous, they didn't seem to belong with the rest of him' (p. 39). Although the event seems quite horrific when considered superficially, Barker strongly suggests that it has served a useful purpose for Burns, bringing him some measure of peace. When he remembers it later, it is as a beautiful scene, with the feathers of a dead magpie shining 'sapphire, emerald, amethyst' (p. 40), causing him to feel that 'he could stay here forever' (p. 40).

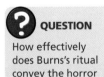

QUESTION

How effectively does Burns's ritual convey the horror of war?

The chapter finishes with emphasising again how important Rivers becomes to the men he treats; the result of the way in which he cares for them more than he does for himself. Although obviously exhausted, he stays up to sit by Burns's bed as he sleeps – a surprisingly maternal image that involves Rivers in Barker's investigation into the way in which war affects masculine roles and identities.

GLOSSARY	
28	flail both a weapon and an agricultural instrument, composed of a handle with a length of wood or chain attached
28	lady's corsets a female undergarment made from fabric ribbed with bone or metal. Laced tightly, it gives the wearer an exaggerated 'hourglass' shape
28	strait-waistcoat old-fashioned term for a strait-jacket, used in hospitals and prisons to confine violent patients
28	post-mortem apron worn by a doctor performing the dissection of a dead body
29	emasculating taking away a man's sense of masculinity or maleness
29	Freudian Johnnies a slightly contemptuous term for doctors who support the ideas of Freud
30	amputations the severing of injured limbs
30	Étaples small town in France that acted as a medical centre during the First World War
30	CCS Casualty Clearing Station; hospitals situated behind the front lines, to which injured soldiers from the battlefield were taken for emergency treatment
30	haemorrhage drastic loss of blood
31	public health the assessment of the health of a community and the development of schemes to improve it. Rivers's point is that it would be a job that would enable Anderson to use his medical knowledge without having to treat patients
32	shrapnel metal fragments from a shell casing that become lethal projectiles when the shell explodes
34	rhetoric skill in using speech as an instrument of communication or persuasion
34	Hyde Park a large park in Central London
34	Serpentine a lake in Hyde Park
35	Marlborough English public school
35	Cambridge Cambridge University
37	clippie bus conductor, who sold and checked passengers' tickets
38	shells hollow metal projectiles containing explosives or gas
39	genitals sex organs

CONTEXT

Richard Dadd (1817–86) (p. 34) was an English painter noted particularly for his pictures of fairies. He is also famous for murdering his father, although Sassoon is incorrect when he tells Rivers that Dadd drowned him in the Serpentine. In fact, he cut his father's throat on a trip to Cobham, Kent, on 28 August 1843. In recognition that the murder was the act of an insane man, Dadd was committed to an asylum, and remained in mental institutions for the rest of his life.

CHAPTER 5

- Rivers meets a new patient, Billy Prior.
- Robert Graves leaves Sassoon alone at Craiglockhart.
- Rivers has a nightmare and analyses his own dream.

As Rivers is checking his patients for the final time before going to bed, the night nurse on duty asks him to see a new admission, Second-Lieutenant Prior, whose nightmares are keeping his roommate awake. Prior cannot talk, so conducts a conversation with Rivers by writing on a notepad. Throughout the interview, Prior is sulky and uncooperative, and concludes it by turning his face to the wall and refusing to write anything more.

Graves says goodbye to Sassoon on the station platform. When Sassoon half-jokingly offers to exchange places with him, Graves accuses him of adopting a superior attitude towards those who break down. Such a differentiation is cruel, he argues, since all soldiers have come close to mental collapse. As Sassoon walks back to the hospital, he regards the civilians around him with disgust, but also faces the uncomfortable realisation that he is experiencing 'pure joy' (p. 44) at being in a place of physical safety.

Rivers returns to his rooms exhausted, and wakes in the early hours of the morning expecting to feel blood on his left arm. When he finds none, he realises that he has had a nightmare, and immediately writes down an account of the dream, in which he recalls experiments he conducted before the war with his colleague Henry Head into the regeneration of nerves. The original experiment was conducted upon Head by Rivers, but in the dream their positions become reversed, and Head begins to cut Rivers's forearm. This causes Rivers to question how far he is prepared to make his own patients suffer in order to achieve a cure.

COMMENTARY

This is a very significant chapter in *Regeneration*, for two reasons. First, it introduces Billy Prior, who is the central fictional character

CHECK THE BOOK
More information about Rivers's life and career can be found in the biography *W.H.R. Rivers* by Richard Slobodin, first published in 1978. Barker cites it as a source for the final book of the *Regeneration* trilogy, *The Ghost Road*, which provides further details of his anthropological research.

not only in this book, but in the *Regeneration* trilogy as a whole. Second, it is here that Barker begins to explore the theme that gives the novel its title: that of regeneration.

Prior's importance to the **narrative** is indicated in the exchange he has with Rivers. The reader has already seen Rivers at work, witnessing his skilled manipulation of speech and silence in order to bring his patients to moments of self-understanding. Such techniques don't work with Prior, however. For a start, Prior is unable to speak, which means that he cannot converse with Rivers properly. Instead, he writes his part of the dialogue on a notepad. The fact that he writes in capital letters makes his comments appear aggressive, as if he were shouting – and this is not an inaccurate impression. From the beginning, he is extremely defensive, and will not answer any of Rivers's questions properly. Finally, he opts out of the interview completely by simply refusing to write anything more at all; an obvious refusal to accept Rivers's authority.

This clearly has an effect on Rivers himself, and for the first time we see him behaving abruptly, even slightly callously, towards a patient. He runs a teaspoon along the back of Prior's throat to test whether he has any loss of sensation that might account for his dumbness, and when Prior chokes and tries to push his hand away, Rivers refuses to accept that he feels pain, only that it might have been 'uncomfortable' (p. 42). He further attempts to establish his superiority over Prior by correcting his spelling.

There is a direct link between this sequence and Rivers's nightmare in which he relives the experience of causing pain to his friend Henry Head in the course of their experiments – although, interestingly, it is a connection that Rivers himself fails to see. When he recalls the patients whose suffering he finds difficult to witness he thinks of Sassoon and Burns, but not Prior.

It is in Rivers's dream and his subsequent contemplation of its meaning that the theme of regeneration enters the novel. What Rivers and Head discover in their experiments on the mending of nerves is that such injuries tend to get more, rather than less, painful before they eventually heal. This is in accordance with Rivers's

 CHECK THE NET
A clear and informative essay on the causes and treatment of shell-shock can be found on the BBC First World War website. Go to **www.bbc.co.uk** and type 'shell shock during world war one' into the search box.

belief that his patients have to suffer as an inevitable part of the process of recovery. Nevertheless, his reluctance to cause his friend pain is mirrored in his discomfort at witnessing the agonies endured by his patients. For further discussion of this passage, see **Extended commentaries – Text 1.**

CONTEXT

On pages 45–6, Rivers uses technical terms for the two stages of nerve regeneration he and Head identified. **'Protopathic'** (p. 45) is a general sensation of pain, or a sensation that is not confined to the specific site of injury. Rivers and Head theorised that this was the first stage of nerve regeneration. **'Epicritic sensibility'** (p. 46) is sensitivity to pain or changes in temperature that is confined to the site where the stimulus is located. For Rivers and Head, this was the second, more advanced, stage of regeneration.

GLOSSARY

41	supercilious arrogant, disdainful
42	analgesia inability to feel pain
43	wound stripe a badge awarded to soldiers wounded in combat which was sewn onto the left forearm of the uniform jacket
44	Armageddon in Christian belief, the site of the final battle between God and Satan that marks the end of the world
44	Golgotha site of Christ's crucifixion
44	*Man* a journal of anthropological research published by the Royal Anthropological Institute of Great Britain and Ireland between 1901 and 1994
44	permutations sequence of combinations
45	militarism a policy of aggressive military preparedness
45	St John's a Cambridge college
45	incision a cut made to the body during a surgical or medical procedure
45	hypersensitivity abnormally sensitive
46	Henry Head (1861–1940), English neurologist who specialised in research into sensation
46	preconceptions prejudices
46	radial nerve one of the main nerves in the arm
46	regeneration renewal or regrowth
47	doctrinaire the upholding of an idea regardless of its practicality

CHAPTER 6

- Rivers has his first formal interview with Prior and another consultation with Sassoon.
- Rivers's work is interrupted by an unexpected visit from Prior's father, followed almost immediately afterwards by Prior's mother.
- Rivers finds Prior alone in the common room fighting the onset of an asthma attack, and settles him for the night as comfortably as he can.

Prior arrives for his first formal consultation with Rivers. Although his ability to speak has returned in the night, he is as antagonistic as he was before. Rivers tries to persuade Prior to speak about the experiences that have caused his breakdown, but Prior claims to only remember the first six months of his period in France. Eventually, tired of Prior's aggressive attitude, Rivers threatens to conclude the interview after only twenty minutes. This shocks Prior enough to make him answer Rivers's questions more fully.

In his meeting with Rivers, Sassoon begins by talking about his associations with pacifism. He denies that he was persuaded to write the Declaration by Bertrand Russell, arguing that 'I am capable of making up my own mind' (p. 53). He identifies Edward Carpenter, whom he had met before the war, as a far more influential figure in his life. But it is Carpenter's theories on sexuality, rather than his pacifist beliefs, that have been most important to Sassoon. He also denies that another influential pacifist he knows, Robert Ross, has had any influence over his actions. Because of Ross's reluctance to publicly support controversial ideas, Sassoon has not even shown him the Declaration.

In the afternoon, Rivers tries to catch up on his paperwork, but suffers a succession of interruptions. Both of Prior's parents come to see him one after the other, which Rivers finds annoying, but uses as an opportunity to find out more about his difficult new patient. Mr Prior does not appear to be very supportive of his son, seeing

QUESTION

Compare Rivers's exchange with Prior to his conversation with Sassoon. What devices does Barker use in order to convey the two men's different characters, attitudes and backgrounds?

Prior's breakdown as a symptom of weakness, while Prior's mother is worried about her son's asthma and apologetic about her husband's insistence on seeing Rivers.

That evening, Rivers finds Prior sitting alone in the patients' common room. The other patients are in the hospital cinema watching a Charlie Chaplin film, but the smoke of their cigarettes has triggered Prior's asthma. Rivers takes Prior up to his room, and makes sure he is settled for what Rivers knows will be a painful night struggling to breathe.

COMMENTARY

In this chapter, Barker begins to develop her portrayal of Prior, providing important details regarding his personal history and family background. In his first proper consultation with Rivers, he initially puts on the same performance as he did the night before; the fact that he has now recovered his voice makes little difference to his generally combative attitude. As in the doctor/patient conversations we have already witnessed, the dominant **point of view** is that of Rivers, and the chapter charts his growing exasperation with Prior's refusal to cooperate. When, for example, Prior claims that he would rather have been admitted to a hospital 'further south', it is followed by an untypical, but heartfelt, comment transmitted directly from Rivers's mind in the first person: 'So would I' (p. 49).

Nevertheless, Barker is aware of the humorous possibilities that open up when Rivers encounters a patient who refuses to play along with his therapeutic methods. Prior refuses to accept that it is Rivers's role to ask questions, and his to answer them. As he says, 'I don't see why it has to *be* like this anyway' (p. 50). For the first time we see Rivers being subject to interrogation, and disclosing details about himself to a patient. And unlike Rivers's other patients, Prior isn't afraid of letting a silence stretch out, forcing Rivers to end it himself.

This does not detract from the fact that, under the antagonistic performance, Prior's trauma is evidently real, and the knowledge that he needs help is underlined by his reaction to Rivers's attempt

---

CONTEXT

Charlie Chaplin (1889–1977) was a British-born comic actor and early Hollywood movie star best known for his hapless comic creation 'the little tramp'. He was working in the United States when the war broke out, and was criticised in some quarters for not returning to join the war effort. However, films he made during the war, such as *Making a Living* (1914) and *Easy Street* (1917), were extremely popular, and were widely shown in order to raise public morale.

to end the consultation early. When he realises that Rivers is completely serious, Prior begins to cooperate, surprising Rivers by his 'sudden capitulation' (p. 52).

Rivers's meeting with Sassoon immediately follows his interview with Prior, inviting the reader to compare the two. With his articulate and thoughtful responses to Rivers's questions in clear contrast to Prior's combative reactions, Sassoon appears in many ways to be a model patient. Although the superficial subject of this consultation is the origins of Sassoon's pacifism, it actually becomes a conversation about something completely different: sexuality.

This remains, though, nothing more than a subtext, recognised by both men, but fully acknowledged by neither. Edward Carpenter's book *The Intermediate Sex* (1908) deals with the topic of homosexuality, and when Sassoon claims that reading it 'saved' his life (p. 54) he is as good as admitting his actual sexual orientation. The fact that Rivers has also read it hints that he, too, may have similar leanings. In this context, Sassoon's mention of Robert Ross, 'a close friend' (p. 54) of the writer Oscar Wilde, is particularly significant, as it indicates that there is still a danger in publicly admitting to being a homosexual. Ross remains anxious to avoid a similar controversy to the one that faced Wilde in 1895. References to such figures indicate the extent to which homosexuality remains encoded within the text, rather than represented openly. Rivers recognises the allusions to Carpenter, Ross and Wilde, but if he had not, Sassoon would not have given away any intimate information.

> **CONTEXT**
>
> Oscar Wilde (1854–1900), was an Anglo-Irish writer particularly known for his witty plays. Convicted of the then offence of homosexuality in 1895, he was sentenced to two years hard labour, and died only three years after his release.

Having learnt something about Sassoon's sexual identity, we then go on to discover further details about Billy Prior. What the separate intrusions of Prior's father and mother into Rivers's office reveal is, first, Prior's class origins and, second, his problematic relationship with his parents. The fact that Prior may not conform to the stereotype of the upper-class officer has already been hinted at in Rivers's observation that he has a 'Northern accent' (p. 49), but now he discovers that Prior's mother taught him to be ambitious to rise above his working-class roots. Mr Prior does not approve, arguing that it has made his son 'neither fish nor fowl' (p. 57). Although Prior physically resembles his mother rather than his father, with

QUESTION

How does *Regeneration* portray the institution of the family?

whom he appears to have an uncomfortable relationship, and has certainly become everything his mother wished him to be, Mrs Prior admits that Billy and his father agree on one thing. Both blame her for alienating Billy from his background.

These discussions help Rivers to see Prior in a different light, emphasised in the scene when he finds him alone in the common room. For the first time, he appears vulnerable, his solitude indicative of his inability to fit into his environment. Although he has left the cinema because the cigarette smoke has brought on an asthma attack, it also suggests his difference from the other officers. Prior is anxious that his asthma might mean that he has to leave Craiglockhart for another hospital, which is a reversal of his earlier claim that he doesn't want to be there, and an indication that he is finally beginning to trust Rivers.

GLOSSARY		
49	sibilance	emphasis on 's' or 'sh' sounds
50	neurasthenic	someone suffering from neurasthenia
50	deep reflexes	involuntary muscular contractions
50	can-can	a high-kicking dance
50	lumbago	lower back pain
50	ostentatiously	exaggeratedly, showily
51	empathic	able to imaginatively experience another's feelings
51	hypnosis	placing a subject in a focused and highly suggestible state
52	capitulation	surrender
52	No Man's Land	the area separating the Allied and German lines on the Western Front, and hence the site on which battles were fought
52	rationale	reason
52	steps	in the context of the Western Front, this signifies the 'fire steps' built into the wall of the trench. Sentries stood on the steps in order to see over the lip of the trench, enabling them to spot any signs of enemy activity
53	Lewis guns	machine guns

53	Edward Carpenter (1844–1929), a writer, philosopher and socialist radical who lived openly as a homosexual at a time when to do so was illegal
54	neuter sexless
54	Robert Ross (1869–1918) lifelong friend of Oscar Wilde, and executor of his estate. Like Carpenter, he was known to be a homosexual
57	short shrift to brush off, treat carelessly
59	three stars insignia of a Captain in the British Army, worn on the shoulder of the tunic
59	chamber orchestra a small classical orchestra
60	housemartins species of bird
61	bar-room socialist someone who only voices his or her left-wing political views when they are drunk

CHAPTER 7

- Prior begins to tell Rivers about his army experiences, but Rivers refuses his request to be hypnotised in order to recover his memory.
- Details of Sassoon's case are published in *The Times*, and Rivers writes his admission report.
- Rivers explains to his colleague Brock how he plans to persuade Sassoon to return to the front.

Sassoon is awoken before dawn by the sound of someone screaming. In the course of a conversation between Rivers and Prior that takes place later that morning, it becomes evident that it was Prior's screams that disturbed him. However, Prior claims that he cannot remember the dream that caused him such distress.

In spite of the events of the previous chapter, Prior's relationship with Rivers remains difficult, and he still cannot resist antagonising him. Rivers becomes slightly uneasy about Prior's growing personal interest in him, noting that he is even reading an anthropological

CONTEXT

In *War Neuroses and Shell Shock*, published in 1919, Fredrick Walker Mott and Christopher Addison observe that 'Whereas hysterical signs and symptoms are common in soldiers and non-commissioned officers they are comparatively infrequent in officers' (p. 188).

study Rivers has written. Prior emphasises that he has never conformed to the upper-class expectations of his fellow officers, and that he regards the army's preoccupation with social distinction as ridiculous. He insists that he wants to be hypnotised in order to help him to remember, but Rivers is of the opinion that hypnosis can cause more harm than good, and is only willing to try it as a last resort.

He then has a meeting with Sassoon, and reads a newspaper report detailing the reading of the Declaration in the House of Commons. Realising how isolated Sassoon feels, Rivers offers to recommend him for membership of the Conservative Club, and rearranges his subsequent consultations for the evenings in order to give him time during the day to play golf.

The Medical Officers have a meeting that evening at which they discuss their cases. Rivers reports that he does not believe that Sassoon is suffering from shell-shock. Although some of the other doctors think that this means Sassoon should merely be left alone for the rest of his time in Craiglockhart, Rivers argues that his job is to actively persuade Sassoon to reject his emotional response against the war and come to the rational conclusion that it is his duty to return to active service.

COMMENTARY

Rivers's evolving relationship with Prior is the main focus of this chapter. Prior persists in asking him questions, and even though he clearly understands why Rivers strives to remain detached, he keeps trying to draw him into a more personal interaction. The events of the previous day have obviously heightened Rivers's awareness of Prior's lower-class origins, and Prior takes great delight in surprising him with his knowledge of Freudian theories, revealing Rivers's automatic assumption that a man from his background would be ignorant of such things. Yet he does not claim any affiliation with the officer class, as is evident from his disdain at the irrelevant myths of military heroism that he was exposed to in officer training.

CHECK THE BOOK

Alfred Lord Tennyson's 'The Charge of the Light Brigade' (1854) (p. 66) describes an event that took place at the Battle of Balaclava during the Crimean War (1853–6) – a disastrous British cavalry charge towards the Russian artillery. In the context of the First World War the poem not only celebrates a brand of heroism that could only be regarded cynically after the massive losses of battles such as the Somme, but also depicts a style of warfare that was no longer possible in such a heavily technological conflict.

The other topic that preoccupies their discussion is sex. First, Prior attempts to embarrass Rivers by drawing him into a conversation regarding his description of sexual practices in India in his anthropological study *The Todas*. He then returns to the subject a little later when he recalls the lines of men outside the brothels at Amiens, and emphasises his own refusal to pay for sex. This aspect of the conversation has a useful function, since it appears to establish Prior as the only character encountered thus far who is not suffering from some kind of sexual confusion.

In Chapter 6 we have already seen Barker placing a conversation with Sassoon directly after a conversation with Prior, implicitly inviting the reader to compare the two men. She does it again here, a tactic which allows her to amplify particular themes regarding class, in particular. Rivers has been somewhat wrong-footed by Prior, who has taken mischievous satisfaction in refusing to conform to his expectations, and now we see him relating to someone more obviously of his own class. He offers to recommend Sassoon for membership of his own club, and organises their subsequent consultations around his golf schedule, which implies a certain fellowship of feeling between them. This is also evident in the continuation of their unspoken recognition of Sassoon's homosexuality. The actual word has not been uttered by either of them, yet when Rivers assures Sassoon that he will not record any 'intimate details' (p. 70) in his admission report that is exactly what he means.

Rivers's defence of Sassoon in the Medical Officer's meeting is thus to be expected, yet he also emphasises his own innately conservative view of the war. He does not approve of the emotional response that has initiated Sassoon's pacifist protest, and argues to his colleagues that it is his role to engage Sassoon in rational debate in order to remind him of his duty. Brock is described in terms which emphasise his coldness and detachment – Rivers thinks that he 'always looked frozen. Even his voice, high, thin and reedy, seemed to echo across arctic wastes' (p. 73) – and he turns Rivers's own medical terminology against him in order to suggest that he may be becoming a little too involved in Sassoon's case.

CHECK THE BOOK

Prior's assertion that he does not pay for sex is something to which Barker returns in *The Eye in the Door*, where we learn of Prior's bisexual preferences, and his past as a male prostitute. Referring back to this conversation, Prior reflects that 'No doubt Rivers had thought it rather silly, a young man's ridiculous pride in his sexual prowess, his ability to "get it" free. But it was nothing to do with that. Prior didn't pay because once, some years ago, he had been paid, and he knew exactly how the payer looks to the one he's paying' (p. 8).

GLOSSARY

63	cacophony a loud and meaningless mixture of sounds
63	Wester Hill meaning 'Western Hill', one of the two hills around which the Craiglockhart area is built (the other is Easter – 'Eastern' – Hill)
65	negative transference identifying the psychoanalyst with a person towards whom the patient feels hostility
65	*The Todas* Rivers's study of the aboriginal Toda people of southern India, published in 1906
65	anthropology the study of human language and culture
66	*The Seat* phrase referring to riders' balance on a horse: if they have a 'good seat', they will not fall off
67	limber two-wheeled gun carriage
67	Amiens town north of Paris
69	road to Calvary in the Bible, the route Christ walked to the site of his crucifixion, carrying his cross on his back
72	chivalrous honourable and courteous, particularly towards women
72	Brock Dr A. J. Brock, a classicist and sociologist, who believed in the importance of engaging traumatised patients in structured activities. He was also Wilfred Owen's doctor at Craiglockhart
74	devil's advocate someone who takes the opposing position in an argument, even if they don't agree with it

CONTEXT

St George is the patron saint of England, whose saint's day (St George's Day) falls on 23 April. It can be deduced that Prior broke down in the course of the Second Battle of the Scarpe, which was fought on 23–4 April 1917: it was part of the Battle of Arras, which took place between 9 April and 16 May 1917.

CHAPTER 8

- Prior describes to Rivers the events leading up to his loss of memory.
- Sassoon and Owen meet for the first time.
- Sassoon plays golf with Anderson.
- Prior goes to Edinburgh for a night out and meets Sarah Lumb. He takes her for a drink, and they talk, but she resists having sex with him.

Three weeks have elapsed since the ending of the previous chapter of *Regeneration*, and Rivers is still trying to get Prior to remember what happened to him in France. The last day he can recall is 23 April, when his company was involved in an attack on the German trenches, and he describes the events of that day in detail in terms that makes it appear ridiculous, even laughable. Rivers does not believe that Prior could have been as detached as he makes out, and asks him to describe his feelings. He suspects that Prior does have some consciousness of what happened, but doesn't want to confront it. However, when he tries to push him further, Prior startles him with the strength of his emphatic assertion that he remembers nothing at all.

A young man with dark hair enters Sassoon's room holding five copies of Sassoon's collection of poetry, and asks him to sign them. He asks for the first to be dedicated to his mother, Susan Owen, which surprises Sassoon, who considers that his frank representation of the horrors of the front might not be suitable for such a woman to read. However, Owen assures Sassoon that he tells his mother everything in his letters anyway. In contrast, Sassoon reveals that he tells his mother nothing in order to protect her from further worry following his brother's death.

Owen is intimidated by Sassoon, but he begins to relax as they engage in an increasingly philosophical debate concerning Christianity and the war. Owen makes a particularly insightful remark about the trenches which engages Sassoon's interest, and when Owen asks him if he would contribute some poems to the hospital magazine, he agrees. Realising that Owen also writes poetry, Sassoon tells him to bring some samples of his work to their next meeting.

Prior goes to Edinburgh for a night out and sees some women in a seedy café as he eats fish and chips. He recognises them as munitions workers, and one of them, Sarah, begins to talk to him. Prior invites her to go to a hotel bar with him for a drink, and as she gets increasingly tipsy she tells him about her boyfriend who was killed in the war, and her reasons for going to work in the munitions factories. Prior and Sarah then walk to a churchyard where he

CONTEXT

Owen's mention of **'Marlborough's army'** (p. 83) is a reference to the War of the Spanish Succession (1701–14), fought between France and Spain on the one side, and Germany, Portugal, England, Holland and Belgium on the other. The armies of England, Holland and Belgium were combined under the command of the British Duke of Marlborough. One of the most important engagements of the campaign was the Battle of Malplaquet, near Mons, fought on 11 September 1709.

begins to kiss and undress her. However, when she won't permit him to go any further, they go their separate ways, agreeing to meet again that Sunday. It is only then that Prior realises that he will not be able to get back to the hospital before the main doors are locked for the night.

COMMENTARY

It is obvious that Rivers has not progressed very far in his attempt to help Prior recover his memory. Their conversation is marked by Prior's hostility and antagonism, and he still takes perverse delight in saying things that will shock Rivers, such as his claim that he experiences war as 'sexy' (p. 78). It is not entirely clear whether Prior is serious about this, but the thought that warfare could be sexually stimulating is nevertheless unsettling. Yet Barker is using Prior here to make a serious point, which is the way in which male aggression is bound up with male sexuality in Western culture, since an ability to fight makes a man appear more masculine, not less. That is why most of the patients at Craiglockhart feel themselves to be inadequate as men, and it makes Prior's retention of a sense of active virility all the more notable.

For the first time in this interview we begin to glimpse the reason behind Prior's extreme defensiveness. Rivers has come to think that Prior suspects that he would be able to remember if he really tried, but is scared to do so. When he suggests that Prior might have at least 'a theory' (p. 80) about what happened, Prior emphatically denies it. His thoughts later in the chapter reveal that he is lying about this, although we do not learn what his theory is.

This is followed by one of the most significant scenes in the novel: the first meeting between Sassoon and Wilfred Owen. Barker presents this in an interesting way, because she does not foreground the importance of the event. At first she does not even reveal the identity of the 'short, dark-haired man' (p. 80) who enters Sassoon's room so tentatively. Indeed, she never introduces him in any obvious way, but merely begins to use his surname once he has incidentally revealed it by asking that one of Sassoon's books be dedicated to 'Susan Owen'. The reason for this is obvious: because Sassoon's **point of view** is the dominant one at this point in the text,

CONTEXT
On 22 August 1917, Owen wrote to his friend Leslie Gunston, 'At last I have an event worth a letter. I have beknown myself to Siegfried Sassoon' (*Wilfred Owen: Collected Letters*, 1967). In contrast, Sassoon in his memoir *Siegfried's Journey 1916–1920* (1945) recalls his first impression of Owen as someone who 'had seemed an interesting little chap but had not struck me as remarkable. In fact, my first view of him was as a rather ordinary young man, perceptively provincial' (p. 58).

we follow his gradual gathering of information about this stranger whom he has never met before. Yet, as in Rivers's reading of Sassoon's poems in Chapter 3, there is an ironic contradiction between Sassoon's ignorance and the reader's knowledge that Owen will write some of the most famous war poems in the English literary canon. Barker can introduce him as a literary character, but our reading of him, just as with Sassoon, will always be influenced by our existing knowledge about the historical figure on which he is based. For a more detailed discussion of Owen and Sassoon's first meeting, see **Extended commentaries – Text 2**.

The final scene in this chapter, narrated from Prior's viewpoint, moves the action out of Craiglockhart and into the streets of Edinburgh, a shift which enables Barker to introduce detailed depictions of women into the text for the first time. Up until this point female figures have been very much in the background, but Sarah Lumb and her friends are assertive, vocal and independent, and do not seem to have much respect for male authority. This is evident not only in their rather crude conversation, but in the way in which Sarah propositions Prior, not the other way around. Through her presentation of Sarah Lumb and her companions, Barker makes us aware of a female contribution to the war effort which gives women an independence that they have never had before. This makes Prior feel slightly insecure, as he thinks this might have been achieved at men's expense: women have 'expanded in all kinds of ways' since the war began, while men have 'shrunk into a smaller and smaller space' (p. 90).

Prior and Sarah's encounter in the graveyard is not only suggestive of the greater sexual freedom enjoyed by women in wartime, but also evokes the theme of memorialisation and remembrance. It is a scene in which Barker's symbolic intentions for *Regeneration* move to the forefront of the text, since for the contemporary reader, Sarah's contemplation of the only partially legible inscription on a tombstone invites an implicit comparison with the lines of names we have seen engraved on war monuments.

QUESTION

When Owen asks Sassoon whether he would describe himself as a pacifist, Sassoon answers 'No' (p. 83). How does this correspond with his adamant antiwar beliefs?

CONTEXT

Many great memorials to the dead of the First World War exist, but perhaps the most striking is the Thiepval Memorial to the Missing on the Somme, which has engraved upon it the names of over 73,000 men whose bodies were never recovered from the surrounding battlefields. It is described by Barker in her 1997 novel *Another World*.

CHECK THE FILM

The 1981 film, *Gallipoli*, starring Mel Gibson, dramatises the campaign from the **point of view** of the Australian troops fighting there.

GLOSSARY	
77	East End working-class area of London
77	billets soldiers' lodgings
77	Beauvois village near the town of St Pol, situated on the road to Arras
77	mess dining hall
78	wire front-line trenches were protected from enemy attacks by lines of barbed wire
79	exultation feeling of extreme joy, rejoicing
81	Gallipoli Turkish peninsula, the site of the Gallipoli Campaign, which took place from 25 April 1915 to 9 January 1916. Sassoon's younger brother Hamo died of wounds on a hospital ship off the coast of Gallipoli in November 1915
82	crucifix stories stories about crosses bearing the figure of the crucified Christ that, seemingly miraculously, remained intact despite shelling
84	flares devices that produce light, but not an explosion, fired from a pistol and used for the purposes of signalling or illumination
86	sleazy dirty or run-down
86	insidious steadily developing towards harm or entrapment
87	yellow tinge caused by exposure to TNT (the explosive substance trinitrotoluene)
87	munitions workers workers in munitions factories, where weapons and ammunition were manufactured
87	pro prostitute
88	Howay (Geordie dialect – see below) hurry up, come along
88	gans over (Geordie dialect) went to
88	Hadaway (Geordie dialect) get lost, go away
89	detonators devices used to trigger an explosion
90	Geordie a term often used to describe all people from the Tyneside area. More specifically, it can indicate only the inhabitants of the city of Newcastle-upon-Tyne
90	Loos Battle of Loos, 25 September–19 October 1915
90	in service working as a domestic servant
91	testimonial reference

93	lichen a plant consisting of fungus and algae living symbiotically, which forms a crust on trees and stone
93	bellyached complained

CHAPTER 9

- Rivers discusses the different shell-shock symptoms exhibited by officers and private soldiers.
- Rivers hypnotises Prior, enabling him to remember the events that caused his loss of speech.
- Rivers contemplates a central paradox of the First World War: the way in which it has encouraged men to form caring relationships with each other in the midst of conflict.

 CHECK THE BOOK

For more information about shell-shock and its treatment during the First World War, see Eric Leed, *No Man's Land: Combat and Identity in World War I* (1979).

The chapter begins with Prior complaining to Rivers that he has been forbidden to leave the hospital for two weeks due to his late return from Edinburgh. He does not want to talk about his amnesia, but instead asks Rivers to explain his opinion that it is unusual for an officer to suffer from mutism. Rivers replies that different ranks exhibit different symptoms: officers tend to stammer, while enlisted men become mute. He theorises that this is due to the fact that the consequences of speaking out in protest would be far more serious for an ordinary soldier than they would be for an officer. Prior points out that Rivers himself has a stammer, but Rivers replies that he has had it from childhood, and thus it cannot be the result of trauma. Prior remains obviously unconvinced, arguing that it shows that Rivers is as ill as any of the men he treats.

That evening, Prior comes to Rivers's office to apologise for his behaviour in their earlier meeting. Realising that Prior is becoming seriously depressed by the nightmares he is suffering as an effect of his repressed memories, Rivers finally offers to hypnotise him. When he does, Prior vividly recollects an incident that took place in the trenches in which two of his men were blown up by a direct shell hit, and he had to shovel their fragmented remains into a bag.

On picking up an intact eyeball with his bare hand he became intensely disturbed and lost the power of speech.

Prior is at first angry, then distressed, at the impact this incident has had on him, and Rivers comforts him while he cries. He confesses that he feels guilt at the loss of men for whom he was responsible, and regards his breakdown as weakness.

Later, when Rivers is getting ready for bed, he thinks about fatherhood and emotional bonds between men. He does not agree with the view that the ability to nurture is inherently female, and finds it ironic that in the course of the everyday life of the trenches, officers develop an almost maternal relationship with the men under their command. Although the soldiers at the front have grown up thinking of war as an inherently '"manly" activity' (p. 108), the static nature of this particular conflict has forced them to adopt a '"feminine" passivity' (p. 108).

COMMENTARY

The chapter begins with a scene that is by now familiar: another meeting between Rivers and Prior, in which Prior is confrontational and uncooperative, and Rivers strives to suppress his irritation and fend off Prior's personal questions and provocative remarks. What is different about this particular consultation, though, is the way in which Barker uses it to provide her reader with information regarding the importance of social class to shell-shock symptoms. Prior's own case implies that class is more of an influence than rank, since even though he is an officer, he has exhibited symptoms characteristic of a private soldier. Thus, his working-class origins have overridden his military status.

This scene also provides one of Prior's most successful attempts to turn the tables on Rivers and make him the focus of interrogation when he makes the point that, while he may not stammer himself, Rivers does. Although Rivers argues that his stammer is different, Prior slyly suggests otherwise. If, as Rivers theorises, a stammer is evidence of a desire to speak in the knowledge that what 'you've got to say is not acceptable' (p. 97), why should it not apply in Rivers's

> **CONTEXT**
>
> In *Annals of Innocence and Experience* (1946), the poet and critic Herbert Read wrote that 'Between the company officer and his men there is every opportunity for the development of a relationship which abolishes all class distinctions and which can have a depth of understanding and sympathy for which I know no parallel in civilian life'.

case? This is another example of Prior's consistent refusal to allow Rivers to occupy the role of detached therapist.

Yet this also paves the way for the moment when Prior surrenders himself completely to Rivers, not only during the hypnotherapy session itself, but also its aftermath. Barker's depiction of his recovery of his lost memories is particularly striking because the reader experiences it alongside Prior. We do not stand outside the event, listening as he formulates his past recollections into a narrative. Instead, we occupy his **point of view** as he relives the episode as if it is happening in the present: a device that makes it appear shocking and immediate.

It is therefore surprising that Prior's main emotion upon coming out of the hypnotic trance is not relief, but disappointment: '*Is that all?*' (p. 104). It is a comment that emphasises the extremities of horror that the soldiers of the First World War endured, where the shovelling of human remains into a bag is regarded as a relatively minor incident. As Prior says, 'I've cleaned up dozens of trenches. I don't see why that would make me break down' (p. 105). When he cries, it is the first time we see him accept Rivers's compassion – even though he does so in an appropriately combative way by 'butting him in the chest, hard enough to hurt' (p. 104).

Rivers's thoughts as he prepares for bed are initiated by that incident, centring as they do upon the subject of men's capability to care for others. The question that preoccupies him is whether the ability to nurture is inherent in men, or whether it implies the adoption of 'feminine' emotions. Although he would like to think that the role of the father has a caring and compassionate aspect, it is clear that he finds it almost impossible to think of such qualities without associating them with motherhood. This perpetuates the theme of masculine crisis by highlighting yet again the irony that it is the war that is causing men to step outside conventionally 'masculine' roles.

> **CONTEXT**
>
> Decomposing bodies were everywhere in the trenches, in spite of attempts to clear them away to try to halt the spread of disease. In her book *Postcards from the Trenches* (1996), Allyson Booth writes that 'Trench soldiers in the Great War inhabited worlds constructed, literally, from corpses. Dead men at the front blended with the mud and duckboard landscape, emerging through the surface of the ground and through the dirt floors of dugouts' (p. 50).

GLOSSARY

95	hymen membrane covering the entrance to the vagina. Traditionally, an intact hymen indicates virginity
96	mutism inability to speak
96	Maghull military hospital near Liverpool, where Rivers worked between 1915 and 1916
96	stammering involuntary pauses or repetitions in speech
98	scythes agricultural tools consisting of a handle and a long curved blade, used for cutting grass or grain
98	Arcadian rustic, simple, peaceful
100	celibate refraining from sexual intercourse
101	gas curtain a heavy curtain hung at the entrance to a dug-out to keep out the fumes from poison gas
102	dugout underground shelter dug into or below the wall of the trench and used as living accommodation for officers
102	funk holes shallow indentations in the trench wall capable of partially sheltering one or two men
102	duckboards wooden planking placed on the floor of the trench in an attempt to protect the soldiers from foot infections caused by constant immersion in water and mud
102	chlorine chloride of lime, added to water in order to kill bacteria
102	fire bay straight sections of trench where troops could line up to shoot their rifles
102	bombardment constant barrage of exploding shells
102	parapets the raised walls of the trench that protected its inhabitants from enemy fire
102	saps narrow tunnels extending out into No Man's Land from the main firing trench
102	work party group of soldiers organised to perform particular tasks, such as transporting ammunition to the front lines, filling sandbags or repairing breaches in the trench wall
103	lime chloride of lime was used extensively in the trenches to prevent infection, in this case from decomposing body parts

CONTEXT

The 'stand-to' (p. 102) was a ritual engaged in by troops in the trenches every morning and evening, in which every man was required to stand on the fire step with his rifle loaded and bayonet fixed in anticipation of enemy attack.

103	gob-stopper large round sweet
104	communication trenches trenches dug at right-angles to the main trenches to allow protected access to the front line
105	wiring party group of men sent out into No Man's Land under cover of darkness to set up or repair the lines of barbed wire that prevented easy access to the trench system
105	erosion process of gradual wearing away
106	texts in this context, extracts from the Bible
106	opaque difficult or impossible to see through
106	John Layard (1891–1974), anthropologist and psychologist who accompanied Rivers on an expedition to Melanesia in 1914
107	*couvade* sympathetic pregnancy, where a man identifies so closely with his partner that he exhibits some of the same symptoms, such as morning sickness
107	mobilization preparation of troops for war

CHECK THE BOOK

In 2001, the BBC broadcast a series called *The Trench*, which recreated life in the trenches of the Western Front with a group of modern volunteers. The story of the project was published in *The Trench: Experiencing Life on the Front Line, 1916*, by Richard Van Emden (2002).

CHAPTER 10

- Sarah's friend Lizzie says she does not want to see her husband, who is hoping to return from France on leave.
- Willard, a patient who suffers from hysterical paralysis, awaits his wife's visit.
- Sassoon and Rivers have dinner at the Conservative Club.
- Rivers meets Willard's wife.

Sarah and her friends at the munitions factory are enjoying a tea break. Sarah can't understand why Prior did not meet her on Sunday as promised. Her friend Lizzie tells the others that her husband has written to tell her that he is expecting to return home on leave, but she does not want to see him. She says that her life has changed for the better since he left, and she intends to go out and enjoy herself in his absence. Sarah thinks she is heartless, but another of the women tells her that Lizzie was regularly beaten by her husband.

The action then returns to Craiglockhart, where Rivers is examining Willard's scars. Willard is unable to walk; he is convinced that his injuries have damaged his spine, and won't admit otherwise for fear of being branded a coward. He is somewhat relieved, though, when Rivers argues that it proves quite otherwise, since a real coward would retain the use of his legs in order to be able to run away.

CONTEXT

Gordon Harbord, a close friend of Sassoon's, was killed at Ypres on 14 August 1917.

Sassoon arrives at the Conservative Club in order to meet Rivers for lunch, and is made uncomfortable by the attention his uniform attracts among the elderly members. He has just learnt that an old friend has been killed in action, and when he lunches with Rivers he confesses that such deaths are making it difficult for him to continue to opt out of the war. He is surprised that Rivers does not exploit his comment in order to mount another challenge to his protest.

When Rivers returns to the hospital, he meets Willard and his wife stranded at the bottom of the drive. Willard is in a wheelchair, and his wife does not have the strength to push him back up the slope. Rivers can see that Willard is furious at his own helplessness, and helps his wife steer the wheelchair back to level ground.

COMMENTARY

The main focus of this chapter is on personal relationships, both good and bad. Sassoon's grief for the loss of his friend Gordon is counterbalanced by Lizzie's pleasure at her husband's absence, and dread at the prospect of his return. With regard to the female characters, the stress is again placed on the opportunities the war has opened up for them: in this case, freedom from abusive husbands. Rather startlingly, Barker reverses our normal assumptions concerning the role of women in wartime, where they are often depicted as anxiously awaiting the safe return of the men they love.

This more negative view of marriage is a theme picked up again towards the end of the chapter, when Rivers meets Willard with his wife. The first time we see Willard, when he is being examined by Rivers, he is presented as a rather threatening figure. In his paralysis he conveys a 'mixture of immobility and power. Like a bull seal dragging itself across rocks' (p. 112), and is described as possessing facial features that are 'strong almost to the point of brutality' (p. 112). When Willard and his wife are together, her deferential attitude towards him is notable: she tries to laugh him out of his bad temper, and looks to him 'for guidance' (p. 119) when Rivers suggests they join him in his office for a cup of tea. By juxtaposing this episode alongside Lizzie's narrative, Barker subtly suggests that this is a woman whom the war has not advantaged, since her husband's illness has denied her any chance of another, more liberated, life outside marriage.

Sassoon's lunch with Rivers is situated in the midst of this analysis of female relationships. Sassoon feels anger at the old men who represent everything he is protesting against, yet he feels his protest to be compromised by his increasing guilt at living the same sheltered existence while his former comrades are being slaughtered. He is surprised that Rivers does not capitalise on these feelings in order to continue his campaign to persuade Sassoon to return to the war. The sections of the chapter focused on Rivers's point of view show that this restraint is not only due to his deeply held conviction that Sassoon should make such a decision himself, but also because he is beginning to realise the effect that dealing with Sassoon is having on his own views. He is particularly worried about the forthcoming Medical Boards at which he will have to decide which of his patients are fit to return to active service. Rivers has always found this stressful, but his regular debates with Sassoon about the validity of the war are bringing his anxieties into the open. Although Prior does not appear in this chapter, we can see the truth of his persistent assertions that Rivers is increasingly becoming directly and personally involved in the issues he is trying to resolve in his patients.

 CHECK THE POEM

Sassoon's anger at seeing the comfortable lives of the elderly men who do not have to fight is echoed in Rudyard Kipling's poem 'A Dead Statesman', which is written from the point of view of a dying politician who anticipates meeting the angry ghosts of dead soldiers in the afterlife.

GLOSSARY	
109	Woodbines popular brand of cigarettes
110	Kaiser Kaiser Wilhelm II (1859–1941), ruler of Germany
111	coal scuttle a bucket containing coal
111	*Requiescat in Pace* Latin for 'Rest in Peace', traditionally a common inscription on grave stones
112	malingering pretending to be ill
113	morning room a room used for relatively informal daytime socialising (as opposed to the smarter drawing room, more commonly used for evening entertaining)
113	watch-chains a chain attached to a pocket watch that could be secured at the other end to a waistcoat or pocket to ensure that it wouldn't be dropped
113	fobs medallions or ornaments attached to a watch-chain
113	saurian resembling dinosaurs
115	View halloa! a huntsman's shout on seeing a fox
115	Eddie Marsh Edward Marsh (1872–1953), at that time Private Secretary to Winston Churchill in the Ministry of Munitions. He was also well known as the editor of five anthologies entitled *Georgian Poetry*, which included early poems by Sassoon
115	geriatric old
115	degenerates individuals who have declined into an inferior state
116	introversion the tendency to be self-absorbed, inward-looking
117	Julian Dadd great-nephew of the painter Richard Dadd, who served with Sassoon in the Royal Welch Fusiliers (see **Detailed summaries: Chapter 4**)
118	Astronomer Royal title given to the Director of the Royal Observatory, Edinburgh
119	stag beetle beetle that derives its name from the antler-shaped mandibles found on the male of the species
119	impotent helpless, or unable to successfully engage in sexual intercourse. Barker is deliberately suggesting both meanings here

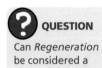

QUESTION

Can *Regeneration* be considered a political novel?

CHAPTER 11

- Sassoon gives a poem to Owen to publish in the *Hydra*.
- Sassoon criticises Owen's poetry, and gives him advice on his writing methods.

Owen visits Sassoon in his room to find him reading a letter from his friend H. G. Wells. In it Wells tells Sassoon that he intends to visit Craiglockhart to talk to Rivers, but Sassoon doubts that he will come. He gives Owen a poem to be published in the *Hydra*, and the two men compare their experience of therapy. Owen says he gets on well with his doctor, Brock, but Sassoon confesses that he often feels intimidated by Rivers's superior intelligence and education.

Owen shows Sassoon some of the poems that he has written. Sassoon comments particularly on the only one that depicts the war, entitled 'The Dead-Beat'. He thinks that it is not very good, but does show potential. He sees that Owen is copying his own style, and advises him that it is not a good idea for a writer to slavishly imitate the poets they admire. He finds another poem, 'Song of Songs', that he thinks is written in Owen's own voice and, much to Owen's consternation, tells him he should publish it in the *Hydra*. He then suggests that Owen continue to work on 'The Dead-Beat', and then bring it back so that they 'can have a go at it together' (p. 124).

COMMENTARY

This is another fictional representation of an actual event, reconstructed by Barker principally from accounts given in Owen's letters. Siegfried Sassoon did indeed act as Wilfred Owen's mentor during the months they spent together at Craiglockhart, and all the poems mentioned in the chapter actually exist.

But this scene also develops some important themes within the novel. In the last chapter, we learnt of Rivers's growing sense of uncertainty regarding his opinion of the war, as well as his view of Sassoon as remarkably introverted and completely uninterested in

 CHECK THE NET

Facsimile editions of the *Hydra*, which include Sassoon's and Owen's poems, can be found in The First World War Poetry Digital Archive at **www.oucs.ox.ac. uk/ww1lit**. Type 'hydra' into the search box.

CONTEXT

Sassoon's joking reference to **'the Onlie Begetter'** on p. 123 is more complex than it appears. Sassoon means 'author', although he is also making a literary reference to the dedication page of Shakespeare's collection of sonnets (1609). The fact that many of the sonnets are addressed to a young man (who may or may not be the 'onlie begetter') subtly adds to Barker's presentation of homosexuality in *Regeneration*.

anyone other than himself. Here, Barker provides evidence of this by revealing that Sassoon has glimpsed nothing of Rivers's internal turmoil; yet she also provides a striking example of him treating another person with consideration and sensitivity.

But this does not mean that Rivers is wrong in his assessment of Sassoon. Sassoon's relationship with Owen is very clearly not one of equals – something he jokingly emphasises to Owen in order to persuade him to publish one of his own poems – and he clearly enjoys taking on the superior role of tutor. His assessment of Owen's work is very definite and not always complimentary: for example, he pronounces 'The Dead-Beat' to be 'not much good', and thinks that some of the words 'could do with changing' (p. 123). Owen does not defend his writing, but defers to Sassoon's opinions in every case. Rivers has already observed that the only thing that brings Sassoon out of his self-absorption is his 'love for his men' (p. 116), and Sassoon is effectively treating Owen just like a military subordinate, even telling him to approach poetic composition 'like drill' (p. 125).

CONTEXT

In *Siegfried's Journey 1916–1920* (1945), Sassoon writes that 'it was not, however, until some time in October, when he brought me his splendidly constructed sonnet *Anthem for Doomed Youth*, that it dawned on me that my little friend was much more than the promising minor poet I had hitherto adjudged him to be' (p. 59).

CONTEXT

Rivers was awarded the Royal Society's highest accolade, the Copley medal, for his achievements in the fields of anthropology and ethnography in 1915.

GLOSSARY

121	H. G. Wells (1866–1946) English novelist, who was a pacifist during the First World War, and supported Sassoon's protest
121	effusions excessive displays of enthusiasm or emotion
122	Gold Medallist of the Royal Society The Royal Society, established in 1660 to promote scientific research in Britain, distributes annual awards to mark significant achievements in various scientific fields
122	Antaeus and … Hercules Antaeus was a giant who challenged Hercules to a wrestling match. Antaeus gained strength from contact with the earth, so could not be defeated by being thrown. Instead, Hercules lifted him above his head until his strength drained away
123	ergotherapy form of treatment promoted by Brock, who made his shell-shock patients engage in mental and physical activity in the belief this would take their minds off their symptoms and so aid their recovery. Brock encouraged Owen in his writing and his editorship of the *Hydra*

> 124   sonnets fourteen-line poems with a set rhyme scheme
> 125   drill military training

CHAPTER 12

- Prior takes Sarah out for the day.
- They have sex, but quarrel later.

Prior turns up at Sarah's lodgings, and although she is initially annoyed at his failure to meet her the previous week, she agrees to go with him on a day-trip to the coast. The only man on the beach who is wearing a military uniform, Prior feels out of place among the holidaymakers who are enjoying the sunshine, and resents their festive mood.

When a thunderstorm begins, he takes shelter with Sarah in some bushes, where they have sex. Afterwards, they go to a pub for a meal, but Sarah takes offence at Prior's adoption of an upper-class accent. Although he is joking, her irritability comes as a relief to him, as he does not want her to think of their encounter in romantic terms.

COMMENTARY

In this depiction of the development of the relationship between Prior and Sarah, Barker examines men's view of women in wartime. Throughout this chapter, Prior's view of Sarah vacillates constantly, moving from uncomplicated lust to something like hatred, then from an almost worshipful adoration to deliberate indifference. He never appears to really want Sarah as a unique individual: instead, he transforms her into a figure who represents his own desires and fears.

At the beach, Sarah becomes the convenient target for the anger aroused in Prior by the sight of civilians enjoying themselves, heedless of the war raging just across the Channel. His feelings

 CHECK THE POEM
Prior's view of Sarah echoes the sentiments expressed in Siegfried Sassoon's poem 'The Glory of Women', which attacks women for their unthinking support for the war while remaining in ignorance of its real horror.

CHECK THE NET

Women were commonly identified with home, family and the natural world in propaganda posters of the time. In one of the most famous, 'Women of Britain Say – Go!' (1915), women watch their men march away to war against a backdrop of green fields and trees; an image that implies to the prospective soldier that fighting for your country and your womenfolk is one and the same thing. The poster can be found on the Imperial War Museum collections website at **www. iwmcollections. org.uk**. Type 'women of britain say go' into the keyword box on the search page.

towards her are extremely threatening: 'She belonged with the pleasure-seeking crowds. He both envied and despised her, and was quite coldly determined to *get* her' (p. 128).

The thunderstorm that strikes so dramatically halfway through the chapter does not only signal the breaking of the hot weather, but also defuses Prior's sense of aggression. There is no suggestion of force in their subsequent lovemaking; instead, Prior appears to be intensely sensitive in his behaviour towards her. However, the fact that he keeps his eyes closed depersonalises the encounter, allowing her to be nothing more than a body to him. In his imagination, it becomes an aspect of nature – Sarah's pubic hair is 'coarse and springy turf' that smells of 'the scent of rock pools at low tide', and she becomes 'a cup from which he drank' (p. 130). Sarah is thus the means by which Prior not only relieves his sexual frustration but also renews himself in a more profound, even spiritual, way.

Poetically described though this episode is, Barker does not allow it to become romantic. Prior is very concerned that Sarah does not think of their liaison as the beginning of a relationship, although Barker implies that he might not really be as callous as he appears. His conscious refusal to admit to himself that 'something had happened that mattered' (p. 131) could imply the opposite: that something has happened that *has* mattered, but he is afraid to confront the implications that this might have for him.

GLOSSARY

127	**ganglion** a cluster of nerves
127	**bloomers** baggy underpants
128	**worm-casts** coils of earth or sand excreted by burrowing worms
128	**sulphurous** reminiscent of the suffocating smell of burning sulphur
129	**marram grass** species of coarse grass that grows on sand dunes

CHAPTER 13

- Rivers has an exhausting day, and that night he finally breaks down. Bryce forces him to take leave.
- Prior recuperates from another asthma attack.
- Sassoon and Owen work on a new poem.
- Sassoon thinks he has been visited in the night by a dead friend, and regrets being unable to talk to Rivers about the experience.

Rivers returns to the novel's centre stage in this chapter, where we see him in the course of a busy and stressful day preparing men for the upcoming Medical Boards, engaging in counselling sessions, attending meetings and dealing with a constant stream of patient complaints and crises.

Prior has returned to the sickbay following a severe asthma attack on the smoke-filled train back from the coast. He is insisting that he has recovered and is now fit for active duty. He feels ashamed at having broken down, and does not want to miss his opportunity to be a member of 'the Club to end all Clubs' (p. 135) – those who have excelled themselves in active service in France.

Anderson has a humiliating reaction to the sight of his roommate Featherstone cutting himself shaving. Featherstone later asks to be moved to another room, as does Prior's roommate Willard, who suspects Prior of being homosexual. Whether sympathetic or not, Rivers knows he can do nothing for either of them, since the hospital is full.

Exhausted, Rivers retires to bed early, but wakes up feeling extremely ill. When Bryce examines him in the morning, Rivers diagnoses himself as suffering from war neurosis, and Bryce insists that he take three weeks' leave immediately.

Evading his own irritating roommate, Fothersgill, Sassoon takes refuge with Owen, where they work together on a new poem Owen

> **CONTEXT**
>
> In his book *A War of Nerves* (2002), Ben Shephard argues that Rivers's therapeutic technique relied heavily on the power of his own personality: 'his patients got better because they wanted to please Rivers, to do what he wanted' (p. 87).

is writing. Sassoon finds the sound of the rising wind distracting, and spends an uneasy night listening to strange noises. He then experiences a strange dream, apparently waking to find a dead friend from his former company standing by the door of his room. The apparition says nothing, then vanishes. Sassoon wants desperately to talk to Rivers about this event, but discovers that he has already left the hospital. It makes Sassoon recall the sense of desolation he felt when his father left the family home, and makes him realise that he thinks of Rivers as a father-figure.

COMMENTARY

This chapter, the last of the second section of *Regeneration*, marks the culmination of one important aspect of the plot. It depicts the moment when the strain on Rivers, which has been suggested since the beginning of the book, finally results in breakdown. The first half of the chapter follows the events of his day in detail, demonstrating not only the sheer volume and variety of the work he does – he is seen acting as a psychotherapist, a physiotherapist, an administrator and an arbiter of disputes between the patients – but also the emotional strain it provokes in him. Every patient requires a different, but equally diplomatic and sensitive, approach. Prior needs, as usual, to be persuaded of Rivers's authority; Anderson's humiliating situation requires tactful care; Willard's prejudices and delusions need to be firmly dealt with.

CHECK THE NET

The facsimile draft of 'Anthem for Doomed Youth', with alterations in Sassoon's handwriting, is part of the Wilfred Owen Digital Archive: **www.hcu.ox.ac. uk**. Type 'anthem for doomed youth' into the search box on the home page and follow the links.

When Rivers realises he is ill, he is also immediately certain of the cause, diagnosing himself, without hesitation, as suffering from war neurosis brought on by constantly listening to the traumatic narratives of his patients. Nevertheless, his 'mutinous' (p. 140) attitude when Bryce immediately removes him from duty shows him being no more cooperative than most of his patients.

The **narrative** perspective then shifts from Rivers to Sassoon, who works with Owen on the draft of a new poem. This is a very good example of the closeness with which Barker has followed historical sources in her portrayal of the relationship between the two poets. Even in an unfinished form, the piece is instantly recognisable to anyone familiar with Owen's work as one of his most famous poems, 'Anthem for Doomed Youth'; furthermore, the alterations she describes Sassoon making are completely accurate. Owen's drafts of 'Anthem for Doomed Youth' still exist, and it is possible to see where Sassoon has crossed out words and replaced them with his own suggestions. Barker's description of the work Sassoon does on the poem in *Regeneration* corresponds exactly to these original alterations.

The last part of the chapter comes to resemble a ghost story, as Sassoon lies in bed that night listening to the rising wind and the mysterious sound of 'tapping, a distinct, purposeful sound' (pp. 142–3). The apparent appearance of one of his dead friends, Orme, by the door of his room is a strange and uncanny event, and Barker leaves it unclear as to how it should be interpreted. Although his strangely unconcerned acceptance of Orme's presence suggests that he is dreaming, Sassoon himself is convinced he is awake. The next morning he makes a clear distinction in his mind between his former horrific shell-shock hallucinations, which 'had come trailing gore' (p. 144), and the calm of the previous night's visitation.

However, the real importance of this event is not whether it is genuine evidence of the supernatural or the product of Sassoon's imagination, but the way in which it causes Sassoon to realise Rivers's true significance for him. His first impulse the next morning is to speak to Rivers, and he is 'unable to account for his sense of loss' (p. 144) when he discovers that Rivers has already left on the early train. This feeling of 'abandonment' (p. 145) triggers a memory from childhood of the day Sassoon's father left his family, and he suddenly understands that Rivers has 'come to take his father's place' (p. 145). Sassoon feels that this is a positive realisation, reflecting that 'if it came to substitute fathers, he might do a lot worse' (p. 145). But while this makes Sassoon feel better, it is nevertheless a rather problematic conclusion in the context of *Regeneration*'s portrayal of fathers as absent, authoritarian or inadequate. If we bear this in mind, then Rivers's role as a paternal figure to his patients may not necessarily be an entirely positive one; a topic that Barker examines in the novel's subsequent chapters.

QUESTION

What devices does Barker use in order to increase the uncanny impact of Orme's appearance in Sassoon's room? Can you think of any other points in the text where she introduces elements of the ghostly or fantastic?

GLOSSARY

132	unconditional discharge release from the army without being required to fulfil any further conditions or obligations
132	orderly a military servant
132	Sam Browne belt a wide belt worn around the waist, with a diagonal shoulder strap attached
133	Trappist reference to a monastic order devoted to a life of contemplative silence
134	battalion canary canaries were used to detect the presence of gas in the trenches and tunnels of the Western Front
134	TB tuberculosis
135	Bolshevik socialist revolutionary
138	claustrophobia fear of confined spaces
138	Theosophist a religious philosophy based on the belief that all religions represent aspects of higher truth. The Theosophical Society was founded in New York in 1875 by Helena Potrovna Blavatsky
138	quartermaster person in charge of obtaining and distributing supplies
140	psychosomatic physical illness with a mental origin
140	sodawater siphon bottle for storing and serving soda water without allowing it to lose its fizz
142	hydro short for 'hydropathic'; an institution offering water therapy, such as spa baths and colonic irrigation. Before being requisitioned for military use during the First World War, Craiglockhart was a hydropathic establishment
143	Lady Bracknellish Lady Bracknell is a character in a play written by Oscar Wilde, *The Importance of Being Earnest* (1895), who possesses an exaggeratedly upper-class manner of speaking
145	father confessor a priest who hears confessions

CHAPTER 14

- Rivers's stay with his brother brings back memories of his childhood.
- Sassoon and Owen continue work on Owen's poem, and Sassoon gives it a title.
- Sarah and Prior meet unexpectedly at the local hospital.
- Rivers goes to stay with his friend Henry Head, and discusses Sassoon's case with Head's wife Ruth during a walk on Hampstead Heath.
- Rivers receives an unexpected job offer.

While visiting his brother, Rivers attends a Sunday service at which he observes the congregation around him and contemplates the images depicted in the church's stained glass windows. He has cynical thoughts about the congregation's unquestioning acceptance of the will of God while young men are dying in France.

Later, while alone in his brother's house, he is reminded of his childhood, and his relationship with his father in particular. A speech therapist as well as a priest, his father spent years trying to cure Rivers of his stammer. Rivers recalls the day when, as a boy of twelve, he eavesdropped on a session between his father and the Reverend Charles Dodgson and concluded that his father's techniques were useless. When, later that summer, he gave a talk on Darwin's theory of evolution that angered his father, the young Rivers was delighted. It proved that, for the first time in his life, his father had listened to something he had said. The older Rivers reflects that he has nevertheless ended up taking his father's place, since it is now he who sits at a desk listening to stammering patients.

The action moves to Sarah, who is accompanying her friend Madge to the hospital, where she is visiting her wounded boyfriend. Feeling excluded, Sarah leaves them alone together, but gets lost trying to find her way out. By mistake, she stumbles into a

CONTEXT

Reverend Charles Dodgson (1832–98) was a British writer, mathematician and photographer, better known as Lewis Carroll, author of *Alice's Adventures in Wonderland* (1865) and *Alice Through the Looking Glass* (1871). Barker elaborates further on Dodgson's relationship with the Rivers family in *The Ghost Road*.

conservatory filled with mutilated men in wheelchairs. Horrified, she hurries away.

Prior is examined by a doctor to assess the condition of his asthma. Bored and annoyed, he leaves the ward and sees Sarah. When she agrees to leave with him, he buys her flowers and kisses her 'on a sudden impulse' (p. 163).

The chapter returns to Rivers, who is now staying in London with his friend Henry Head and his wife Ruth. Head offers Rivers a job as a psychologist with the Royal Flying Corps. Although Rivers is tempted, he tells Head that he would not be able to accept because Craiglockhart is due to be inspected at the end of the month. He knows that the military authorities do not approve of the way in which the hospital is being run, and feels he must remain to give Bryce his support.

COMMENTARY

Up until this point, Rivers has been depicted only in his professional capacity as a psychotherapist. Here, though, we see Rivers in other, more personal, roles – that of brother, son and friend. Learning more about him makes him a more fully rounded character, and also gives Barker the opportunity to complicate the image of the father with which the previous chapter concluded.

When Sassoon imagines Rivers as a father it is a caring and consoling image, but the role of the father takes on much more negative associations in this chapter. Attending church, Rivers finds himself surrounded by a congregation composed of 'old men, and women of all ages' (p. 149) who seem quite happy to resign themselves to the belief that they live in an orderly world controlled by a benign God. Yet for Rivers, the folly of this belief is summed up in the images in the stained-glass windows above his head, which depict Abraham preparing to sacrifice Isaac. Rivers concludes that the son's readiness to surrender himself to his father's will represents '*The* bargain … The one on which all patriarchal societies are founded' (p. 149), which dictates that sons obey their fathers in return for the promise of eventually inheriting their fathers' authority. Rivers regards the war as a perversion of this bargain, since the sons going to the battlefields of the Western Front at their fathers' request will not survive to take their fathers' place. Unlike Isaac, who is saved by divine intervention, they really are sacrificed. In this way, fatherhood becomes something authoritarian and potentially murderous. It is a conclusion subtly underlined by Rivers's awareness of the other image in the window: that of Christ's crucifixion. Although Barker does not explore the implications openly, she leads us towards the realisation that the Christian religion is itself founded upon the sacrifice of a son at the command of a father.

It is Rivers's own father, however, who becomes the ultimate **symbol** of **patriarchal** male authority in this chapter. We learn that he had a 'dual role as priest and speech therapist' (p. 153) – thus, he symbolises both the power of God and the management of language. In treating Rivers's stammer, he assumed a control over his son's voice that was only broken when Rivers came to the conclusion that his father's techniques were nothing more than 'nonsense' (p. 155). This allowed Rivers to symbolically 'kill' his father's authority over him. The final blow to his father's power was when Rivers gave a talk on evolutionary theory which his father was greatly offended by, believing Darwin's ideas to be blasphemous. Previously, Rivers's father had always concentrated on the mechanics of his son's speech without bothering about the content, and this was the first time Rivers had made him actually 'listen to what he had to say, and not merely to the way he'd said it' (p. 155).

Rivers is nonetheless aware that this feeling of separation from his father may well have been an illusion, since he has, effectively, taken his father's place – and not just because he, too, treats stammering patients. The fact that he is attempting to complete a letter to Sassoon when he falls into reminiscences about his childhood draws our attention again to the father–son relationship developing between them. Now, however, we see it in a different light. As Rivers has repeatedly pointed out to Sassoon, his role is to persuade him to return to active service, and although he has no son of his own, he may thus be as guilty as any other father of sacrificing a young man whom he loves in order to maintain his own authority.

CONTEXT

The theory of evolution was developed by the British naturalist Charles Darwin (1809–82), author of *The Origin of Species* (1859). He argued that all life has descended from a common ancestor, and has adapted itself to suit specific environments – a process he termed 'natural selection'. His ideas were controversial because they contradicted the biblical belief that God created man in his own image.

CHECK THE POEM

Wilfred Owen's poem 'The Parable of the Old Man and the Young' retells the story of Abraham and Isaac in the context of the First World War, and comes to the same conclusion as Rivers does in the first part of this chapter. When the old man is given the chance of a substitute for the sacrifice of his son, he refuses, 'but slew his son, / And half the seed of Europe, one by one'.

The following scene between Sassoon and Owen, still working on Owen's poem back at Craiglockhart, is placed in ironic opposition to Rivers's reflections. First, Owen's self-belief has matured to the point where he too is finding his own voice, both on the page and in his exchanges with Sassoon. This growing 'self-confidence to contradict his hero' (p. 157) leads to a lively debate on the theme of sacrifice. Owen refuses to agree with Sassoon's opinion that the loss of life on the battlefields is entirely meaningless, arguing that it is possible to criticise the human cost of war while still feeling 'pride in the sacrifice' (p. 157). He even produces one of Sassoon's poems as evidence that Sassoon does 'exactly the same thing' (p. 157). Although Sassoon unwillingly agrees that it is possible to interpret the poem that way, he thinks there is a danger that it would lead to the possibility of 'making it out to be less of a horror than it really is' (p. 157). Barker's narrative focus has moved from the reflections of the father who sacrifices his son to the perspective of the sons who are being sacrificed, seeing through the poetry of Owen and Sassoon a moving attempt to applaud the courage of the dead while still depicting the horror of war.

Sarah Lumb's encounter with the maimed men in the hospital maintains the chapter's focus on the theme of sacrifice. In *Regeneration*, Sassoon, Prior and Rivers have all experienced moments when they look upon the civilian population as callous and uncaring, carrying on their lives as normal without consideration for the suffering of the soldiers on the battlefields. But what Sarah's experience demonstrates is the way in which such horrors are routinely hidden from view, leaving non-combatants genuinely ignorant of what is actually happening. The soldiers, she realises, have been put in the conservatory 'to get the sun, but not right outside, and not at the front of the hospital where their mutilations might have been seen by passers-by' (p. 160), and her reaction is reminiscent of the anger that motivates Sassoon to write his poetry: 'If the country demanded that price, then it should … be prepared to look at the result' (p. 160).

Sarah's subsequent reunion with Prior provides a more optimistic scene in an otherwise rather bleak chapter. For the first time, their association seems to be based on more than lust – Prior, seeing her, realises that 'he'd forgotten … how much he *liked* her' (p. 162), and his gift of flowers and his kiss are endearingly romantic. However, the 'bitter, autumnal smell' (p. 163) of the chrysanthemums, which fades into the smell of 'burning leaves' mentioned in the opening of the chapter's next scene, reintroduces **motifs** of death and decay which undercut this rare moment of happiness.

The conversation between Rivers and Ruth Head that follows skilfully ties up all the chapter's themes and motifs. The men sitting in wheelchairs 'waiting for someone to come and push them away' (p. 164) that Ruth and Rivers pass on their walk are immediately reminiscent of Sarah's earlier encounter in the hospital. It is after seeing them that Ruth speaks out in support of Sassoon's protest, as if, like Sarah, she has been impelled into a critique of the war by the sight of its hidden victims. The moral complications of Rivers's position are also recalled when Ruth reminds him not only that the job of returning Sassoon to the war is his responsibility, but also of the potentially disastrous consequence of assuming such a role – for Rivers himself, as well as Sassoon.

 **CHECK THE BOOK**

Barker's 2007 novel *Life Class* features a very similar episode, in which the principal female character Elinor describes her feelings on walking past a group of disabled soldiers in wheelchairs: 'I watch them watching me noticing the missing bits, looking at the empty trouser legs, or, equally awful, not looking at them. And I feel ashamed. Just being what I am, a girl they might once have asked to dance, is dreadful. I feel I'm an instrument of mental torture through no fault of my own' (p. 150).

GLOSSARY	
149	the Somme site of one of the most devastating battles of the First World War, fought between July and November 1916
149	the Virgin Virgin Mary, Jesus Christ's mother
149	St John one of Christ's twelve apostles
150	hassocks cushions on which worshippers kneel to pray
151	malaria tropical illness carried by mosquitos
153	the Apostles at Pentecost following Christ's death, his followers were visited by the Holy Ghost, which manifested itself in tongues of fire and caused them to speak in many languages
154	consonant combinations two consonants linked together which combine to form a single sound ('wh' is pronounced as 'w'; 'ph' is pronounced 'f', for example)
154	croquet an outdoors game involving the hitting of wooden balls through hoops with mallets. The fact that Dodgson is involved in the game may also evoke memories of Alice's nonsensical game of croquet in *Alice's Adventures in Wonderland* continued

CONTEXT

The reference to 'Michal's bride-price' (p. 150) is an **allusion** to the biblical story of Michal, who was the daughter of Saul, king of Israel. David wanted to marry her, but could not afford a dowry – a payment given to the father of the bride. Saul, however, did not demand money, but a hundred foreskins taken from his enemy the Philistines. This was not the gesture of generosity it seemed, as Saul was jealous of David and hoped in this way to ensure his death in battle.

155	Bronze Age period of prehistoric society in which humans began working with metal
156	soft thud-thud of the guns the battle fields of France were only just across the English Channel, and inhabitants of the south coast could hear the sound of shelling and firing quite clearly
157	Valhalla in Norse mythology, the hall in the afterworld where warriors go if they die in battle
158	the *Nation* political journal first published in 1906, which supported the pacifist position during the First World War
158	gangrene a common infection of wounds during the First World War, in which the body tissue around the injury begins to die, turning black and developing a strong odour
159	green and hairy reference to the **idiomatic** expression 'playing gooseberry', meaning a person who is with a couple, and thus the outsider
159	incinerator an industrial furnace used to burn waste; in this context, medical waste such as old dressings and amputated body parts
160	Medusa female figure from Greek mythology, who has snakes for hair and a gaze that can turn men to stone
162	puttees woollen bandages wound around the lower part of the legs, and tied off at the top
163	Hampstead Heath large area of parkland in London
163	Ruth Head (1866–1939), wife of Henry Head, and an author and translator in her own right
165	Get thee behind me, Satan Jesus's rejection of the temptations of the Devil

CHAPTER 15

- Rivers visits Burns at his house on the Suffolk coast.
- Rivers wonders why he has always regarded Burns's experience as uniquely horrific when all his patients have endured similarly appalling events.

- Burns disappears from the house in the middle of the night, and Rivers searches for him.
- Burns talks about his experiences in France for the first time. Rivers wonders whether this indicates that he is beginning to recover.

Rivers arrives in Aldeburgh in Suffolk, and Burns meets him at the station. They walk to his house along the beach, and Rivers is surprised that Burns does not seem disturbed by the coils of wire placed on the shingle, which Rivers thinks might remind him of the wire in No Man's Land. In fact, Burns appears to be acting fairly normally, although he is still not eating. Throughout Rivers's stay, he serves no food to his guest.

The next day Rivers and Burns go for a long walk. Rivers had expected to meet Burns's parents during his visit, but Burns tells him that they are still in London. Burns has gone to the house in Aldeburgh to escape from his father, who is 'a great believer in the war' (p. 171). In the course of their walk, they arrive at a 'squat, circular building' (p. 171) surrounded by a deep moat, and Burns remembers how he would play there as a child, drawn to its sinister atmosphere.

 QUESTION

How does seeing Burns in his home environment add to or change our understanding of him?

That evening Rivers continues work on a paper on the repression of war experience that he is due to deliver to the British Medical Association. As he begins to write, he is struck by the thought that he is doing so in the presence of someone who is still strongly repressing the memories of what has happened to him. Rivers realises that, while his whole therapeutic method is based upon the necessity of remembering buried traumatic memories, he has always treated Burns differently. In his own mind, he has made Burns's experience uniquely horrific, whereas in actuality it is probably no more unspeakable than the things that have happened to any of the other officers whom Rivers treats.

The next day is stormy, and Rivers and Burns go for another walk on the beach. Burns is clearly disturbed when they stumble across an area of shingle scattered with 'cods' heads, thirty or more, with blood-stained gills and staring eyes' (p. 176). After a while, though, he seems to have regained control of himself.

That night the storm worsens, and Rivers is awoken by the sound of an explosion. Once he is properly awake, he realises that it is the signal to launch the lifeboat, but is worried about Burns, whom he has heard go downstairs. When Rivers gets up to see if Burns is all right, he finds the house empty. He goes out to look for him, becoming increasingly worried. He finds him in the moat surrounding the tower, staring up at it unblinkingly. Eventually, Rivers manages to get him to walk home.

The next day, Burns begins to speak about his experience of the war for the first time, although he does not directly mention the incident that led to his breakdown. Rivers thinks that this shows that Burns is beginning to place what has happened to him in some sort of perspective, but at the same time is aware that his 'own sense of the horror of the event seemed actually to have increased' (p. 184). He realises how much Burns has been changed by the war, but hopes that he has begun the process of some sort of recovery.

COMMENTARY

The purpose of this chapter is to round off Burns's story, while continuing to trace Rivers's growing dilemma regarding his role in promoting the continuation of the war. Fatherhood remains an important theme, as does the concept of sacrifice.

Landscape also plays a central role in this section of *Regeneration*. As they walk to Burns's house, Rivers's attention is drawn to 'the tangles of barbed wire that ran along the beach' (p. 167), an observation that has the effect of overlying the spectral presence of No Man's Land upon an autumnal British seaside scene. In this way, Barker reproduces in her text the perspective of shell-shocked soldiers such as Burns, whose memories of war form a constant mental backdrop to everything they see and do. Barker continues doing this throughout the chapter – Rivers mistakes the sound of the maroon for a bomb, the cods' heads on the beach recall the bodies of dead soldiers, and the marshes are a 'waste of mud' (p. 179) that remind Rivers of the battlefields of France. What is

CHECK THE POEM

In 'Channel Firing', the novelist Thomas Hardy (1840–1928) describes how the sounds of the big guns in France could be heard across southern England.

even more remarkable, of course, is that these are things that Rivers has never seen first hand, but only through the recollections of his patients.

However, it is the tower that Burns shows Rivers on their first walk that becomes the most obvious example of this tendency of the past to intrude into the present. It is a completely negative image with no redeeming features whatsoever: it is 'a dead place' (p. 171), and 'feels like a place where people have died' (p. 172). When Burns vanishes from the house in the midst of the storm, it is here that Rivers finds him, 'staring up at the tower, which gleamed white, like the bones of a skull' (p. 180). In the middle of a landscape which itself resembles No Man's Land, Burns is confronting the absolute horror of war and the sacrifice that it demands. (For further discussion of the significance of the tower and its associations, see: **Themes: Fathers.**)

Although he himself has recovered from his traumatic symptoms, Rivers has not regained his previous belief that the war must continue to be fought. Burns, for whom he has always felt especially strong sympathy, becomes the most persuasive representative of its **tragedy** and waste. 'He looked up at the tower that loomed squat and menacing above them, and thought, *Nothing justifies this. Nothing nothing nothing*' (p. 180). The chapter ends with Rivers expressing the hope that Burns may continue to recover, particularly since he has begun to talk about his war experiences. However, he also realises that Burns has lost any chance of being the same person as he was before the war.

 CHECK THE POEM
Parallels between the soldier and the betrayed and crucified Christ were common in poetry of the period. Examples include Wilfred Owen's 'At a Calvary Near the Ancre', Rudyard Kipling's 'Gesthemene' and D. H. Lawrence's 'Eloi, Eloi, Lama Sabachthani', the title of which repeats Christ's final words on the cross: 'My God, my God, why hast thou forsaken me?'.

GLOSSARY		
167	naphtha flares	form of lighting fuelled by naphtha, a flammable compound
169	flint-knapping	the ancient art of making stone tools
171	rigging	collective term for a boat's masts, sails and ropes
171	estuary	tidal mouth of a river
171	raids	Zeppelins (navigable balloons or airships) were used to mount bombing raids over Britain between 1915 and 1917

continued

CONTEXT

Jonah (p. 173) was a biblical prophet who tried to ignore God's command to go to and preach in the city of Ninevah. When Jonah attempted to escape by getting on a boat going in another direction, God caused a storm to strike the boat. The sailors, perceiving Jonah was the cause, threw him overboard. In order to save him, God commanded a whale to swallow Jonah. After three days and nights, Jonah repented and God allowed the whale to expel him out onto dry land.

171	Martello tower small two-storey forts built during the nineteenth century for the purpose of defence against possible invasion by sea
174	Tripos term describing the different parts of the degree system at Cambridge University
174	rheumy producing a discharge
174	Melanesians general term for the inhabitants of the islands of New Guinea, Vanuatu, New Caledonia and the Solomon Islands
176	offal waste parts, especially intestines
177	blown eggshell an empty eggshell that has had its contents drawn out through a small hole in the base
177	maroon an exploding flare
178	oilskins waterproof clothing worn by sailors
179	sump holes water-filled hollows in the ground
181	ornithology study of birds
181	palimpsest a surface that has been written on, erased, and written on again
182	dyke ditch
184	chrysalis cocoon in which a caterpillar transforms into a butterfly

CHAPTER 16

- Rivers returns to Craiglockhart.
- Bryce advises him to accept Henry Head's offer of a job, as he does not expect to remain in charge of Craiglockhart much longer.
- Rivers tells Sassoon of a strange event that he experienced on the Solomon Islands. In return, Sassoon tells Rivers of his mysterious encounter with Orme.
- Sassoon shows Rivers another poem, and tells him that he has decided to return to active service.

Rivers arrives back at Craiglockhart following his leave. He speaks with Bryce about the offer of a job he has received from Henry

Head, and Bryce advises him to accept. He thinks that he will be asked to leave his post as Commandant of the hospital following the forthcoming inspection. Rivers says that he probably will take the job, but the thought of leaving Craiglockhart makes him aware of how much he enjoys working there. Although returning to London will allow him to resume the anthropological research his war work has interrupted, he realises that he no longer regards working with shell-shock victims as 'an interruption of his "real" work', but something 'he was meant to do' (p. 186).

In his next meeting with Rivers, Sassoon begins to describe his strange dreams of dead comrades. Seeing that Sassoon is awkward about appearing irrational, Rivers tells him of an incident that happened to him while he was conducting research in the Solomon Islands. The islanders believe that spirits come to a corpse to carry its soul away in a canoe, and when Rivers attended a ceremony for the dead, he heard strange 'whistling sounds' (p. 188) at the moment of the spirits' supposed arrival. Although he is of the opinion that this experience could well have a rational explanation, he can't find one that 'fits all the facts' (p. 188).

In response, Sassoon tells Rivers about Orme and other similar visitations. He does not call these experiences nightmares, since the ghosts aren't threatening. Instead, he says, they merely appear 'puzzled. They can't understand why I'm here' (p. 189). Sassoon has written a poem about them, which he shows to Rivers. Rivers finds it extremely moving, and Sassoon has to tactfully look away while he takes off his glasses to wipe his eyes. He then tells Rivers that he has decided to give up his protest and return to the army, but is not looking forward to confessing this to his pacifist friends. When Sassoon asks Rivers whether he is pleased by his decision, Rivers replies that he is.

COMMENTARY

The chapter begins with Rivers seemingly regaining confidence in his work at Craiglockhart. The prospect of leaving brings him a sense of certainty that what he is doing is right. However, this renewed self-belief is about to be tested by Sassoon. Rivers is deeply affected by Sassoon's poem, which explains Sassoon's decision to

CONTEXT

The poem that Sassoon shows Rivers is called 'Sick Leave', and was included in *Counter-Attack and Other Poems* (1918).

return to the war in profoundly personal terms. The 'extraordinary mixture of love and hostility' (p. 190) with which Sassoon regards Rivers at this moment recalls Rivers's earlier dilemmas regarding the extent of his responsibility for the return of already damaged young men to the front line. When Sassoon asks Rivers if he is pleased with his decision it is both a plea for approval and a challenge. Rivers's answer – 'Oh yes. I'm pleased' (p. 190) – is outwardly affirmative, but Barker provides the reader with no context in which to interpret this statement. A great deal of the novel is **narrated** from Rivers's **point of view**, and we often have an insight into what he is thinking; but here his speech is merely reported, leaving us to make up our own minds about how he really feels.

> **GLOSSARY**
>
> 185   pork-pie hat hat with a flat top and thin brim
> 189   Frise area situated near the Somme in France

CONTEXT

Nancy Nicholson and Robert Graves were married in 1918. Nancy was a painter, fabric designer and ardent feminist. By 1926, she and Graves were living in a *ménage à trois* with another woman, the poet Laura Riding. In 1929, Graves and Nancy separated, and he moved to Mallorca with Laura, although the couple were not formally divorced until 1949.

CHAPTER 17

- Sarah is visited by her mother, who criticises her relationship with Billy Prior and her decision to become a munitions worker.

- Graves tells Sassoon that he has been writing to a girl, and denies that he has ever had homosexual leanings.

- Passing the time while working on the assembly line in the munitions factory, Sarah and her friends discuss the sexual shortcomings of upper-class men and the case of a fellow munitions worker, who is in hospital following a botched abortion.

- Rivers reminds Sassoon of the growing intolerance towards homosexuals, and warns him that he is a vulnerable target.

Sarah's mother Ada arrives in Edinburgh, and Sarah tells her about her relationship with Billy Prior. Ada warns Sarah against having sex with him, partly to avoid the risk of pregnancy, but also because it will mean that, having lost her virginity, Sarah will not be able to find anyone to marry her in the future. She also thinks Sarah should give up munitions work and do something more feminine, such as a job as a waitress or a lady's maid. Sarah reflects on the contrast between how her mother lives her life, and the life she aspires to for her daughters. She wants them to make a respectable marriage, but has an extremely cynical attitude towards men herself. Ada has brought her children up alone and supported them by her own efforts. Sarah has never known her father, who may have 'departed this life, the town, or merely his marriage' (p. 195).

Sassoon and Graves meet for dinner. Sassoon tells Graves that he has told Rivers he will rejoin the army provided his return to France can be guaranteed. Graves, though, is angry with Sassoon for ever having begun his protest. He argues that he promised to serve his country when he joined up, and a real gentleman would not break his word. Sassoon retorts that Graves should remember the cost of the war, and that 'if you had any *real* courage you wouldn't acquiesce the way you do' (p. 198).

Graves reveals that a former close friend of his, Peter, has been arrested for approaching men for sex, then immediately tells Sassoon about his correspondence with a girl, Nancy Nicholson. Graves does this because he does not want Sassoon to think that he is homosexual, or that he ever had indecent thoughts about Peter. Ironically, Peter has now been referred to Rivers to be 'cured' (p. 199).

Sarah joins her friends on shift in the munitions factory. She tells them of her mother's opinion of Prior, and this leads into a discussion of the sexual preferences of upper-class men. One of the other girls worked as a domestic servant before the war, and she says that the son of the family was homosexual. There is general agreement among the women that most gentlemen are inclined that way, or at the very least are completely indifferent towards women.

Noticing that one of the girls is missing, Sarah enquires where she has gone. She is told that she is in hospital, having perforated her bladder trying to bring on an abortion. Ironically, despite the damage she has inflicted upon herself, she is still pregnant.

CONTEXT

Because it was not possible to obtain an abortion in a hospital, women resorted to desperate measures to rid themselves of unwanted pregnancies. All kinds of methods were used, such as hot baths, deliberate falls, the drinking of turpentine and, as in Betty's case, attempts to rupture the cervix with instruments such as knitting needles. It was not until 1928 that abortion became legal, although that was only in cases when the life of the mother was thought to be in danger, and could only be carried out up to twenty-eight weeks after conception.

Back in Craiglockhart, Rivers visits Sassoon, who is due to go before the Medical Board the next day. Sassoon is depressed after his conversation with Graves. He does not like the way Graves has felt the need to distance himself from Peter and any association with homosexuality, since it shows that he finds such behaviour repellent.

CONTEXT

Great social concern was expressed at the beginning of the war about the rise of so-called 'khaki fever': the extreme sexual excitement said to be felt by young women on seeing men in uniform. So serious was the problem perceived to be that women's police patrols were formed in order to enforce decent and modest behaviour between soldiers and young women in public places. For more information, read Angela Woollacot's essay in the *Journal of Contemporary History*, '"Khaki Fever" and Its Control: Gender, Class, Age and Sexual Morality on the British Homefront in the First World War' (April 1994).

Rivers says that Peter was lucky to have avoided prison, observing that intolerance against homosexuality is on the rise. He does not find this surprising, arguing that in a time of war, men are naturally thrown into intimate, even loving, associations with each other, which makes it necessary to separate the 'right' kind of love from the 'wrong' kind. One of the reasons that he is pleased that Sassoon has decided to give up his protest is because to continue it might well make him vulnerable to persecution on the grounds of his sexuality. When Sassoon says that he finds conforming to society's expectations unacceptable, Rivers retorts that it is about time he 'grew up' (p. 205).

COMMENTARY

This chapter is an excellent example of Barker's use of multiple perspectives to focus on a single theme. Its central preoccupation is with sexuality; a topic Barker develops by keeping the narrative point of view moving between two extremely different social groups – working-class women and upper-class men – who never encounter each other directly, and whose experiences and opinions differ absolutely.

The conversation between Sarah and her mother with which the chapter opens is centred upon the sexual standards that society sets for women. Ada does not disapprove of Sarah's liaison with Prior on moral grounds, but because it means she is risking becoming pregnant while unmarried. In her opinion, men will be more keen to marry Sarah if she withholds her sexual favours, and Ada bluntly tells her that 'You're never gunna get engaged till you learn to keep your knees together' (p. 194). Ada is ambitious for her daughters to make good marriages, but is scornful of what she sees as romantic delusions. Instead, she regards the relationship between the sexes as resembling that between predator and prey or parasite and host: 'In *her* world, men loved women as the fox loves the hare. And women loved men as the tapeworm loves the gut' (p. 195).

Ada herself lives an independent existence without a man, but Barker hints at the effort required to maintain herself and her daughters – she is doing no more than 'scratching a living together' (p. 195), and Sarah feels 'pain' at the sight of her 'thin, lined hands' (p. 196). It is easy to assume that Ada is a living contradiction to the advice she gives her daughter, but she is not. Instead, she represents the struggle that is required of a woman who lives her life alone, and it is a fate she does not wish her own daughters to share.

In the meeting between Sassoon and Graves that immediately follows this episode, the narrative switches both the gender and the class of the main characters. Yet the topic of their conversation becomes the same: the issue of what constitutes the 'right' kind of sexual behaviour. Graves is upset at the news that a former friend has been arrested for homosexuality, and it is this event that motivates him to emphasise to Sassoon that he is definitely heterosexual. When Graves describes his correspondence with Nancy Nicholson as proving that his 'affections have been running in more normal channels' (p. 199), he is voicing his society's belief that homosexuality is a perversion. It is evident that he does not pause to consider what effect such a statement might have on Sassoon.

In the light of this conversation, the banter among the female munitions workers on the assembly line is very ironic. Unlike Graves, the women are not disgusted by homosexuality, but rather see it as an inevitable failure of masculinity caused by the effete lifestyle of the upper classes. Memories of the exchange between Sarah and her mother are also evoked in the story of Betty, who has damaged herself trying to abort an unwanted baby. This demonstrates that, for a working-class woman, practising heterosexuality can be as risky as active homosexuality is for an upper-class man.

The growing risk of being homosexual in Britain in the First World War period is emphasised to Sassoon by Rivers. When men are

CONTEXT

In *Goodbye to All That*, Graves writes that 'in my fourth year I fell in love with a boy three years younger than myself, who was exceptionally intelligent and fine-spirited. Call him Dick'. Graves is careful to stress, though, that 'I was unconscious of any sexual desire for him' (p. 45).

thrown closely together in a military situation, he argues, it is necessary to police their relationships particularly closely. His retort when Sassoon asserts that he will live his life the way he wants to is surprisingly blunt, though. In telling Sassoon 'It's time you grew up. Started living in the real world' (p. 205), he sounds like a father scolding a son – an observation that brings the chapter full circle. Rivers, like Ada, is acting as the voice of adult pragmatism, trying to persuade his child of the necessity of conforming to acceptable social standards of sexual behaviour.

GLOSSARY

193	Princes Street	main shopping street in Edinburgh
193	them factories	factories that produce condoms
194	anaemic	having a lack of iron in the blood, which causes tiredness and pallor
194	tapioca	milk pudding
195	black bombazine	fabric used to make mourning clothes, and thus associated with widows
195	tapeworm	a parasitic worm that can be introduced to the body in undercooked food, then grows in the digestive tract
197	niblick	a type of golf club
197	War Office	until 1963, the government department responsible for the administration of the army
199	soliciting	approaching people and offering them sexual services
203	platonic	non-sexual
204	Charterhouse	English public school
205	tilting at windmills	attacking imaginary enemies; taken from Cervantes's 1604 novel *Don Quixote*, in which the hero attacks windmills while imagining them to be giants

CHAPTER 18

- Prior goes before the Medical Board, and is disappointed to be only passed fit for home service.
- Sassoon gets impatient, and walks out before his turn in front of the Board.
- Rivers is furious with Sassoon, but relieved to hear that he has not changed his mind about going back to the army.

Rivers watches Prior sitting in front of the Medical Board, and perceives that he is caught up in an agonising dilemma. While he genuinely desires to return to active service in France, part of him also wants desperately 'to save his life' (p. 206) by remaining at home. When Prior is asked directly by one of the Board members whether he feels fit enough to return to active service, he cannot answer and remains silent.

Sassoon is waiting for his turn to go before the Board, but realises that it is running behind schedule, making him late for a social appointment. He is tired after a sleepless night caused by a letter from the Quartermaster in his former battalion asking Sassoon when he is going to return. It has made Sassoon feel as if he should 'rush back to France at once' (p. 207). Eventually, he loses patience, and leaves the hospital.

After the Boards are over, Rivers visits Prior in his room, where he finds him in tears. He is both upset and furious that he has not been passed fit for active service abroad, although Rivers tries to make him see that his asthma is a genuine problem that could endanger not just his life, but also the lives of the men under his command. Prior turns his frustration and sense of failure on Rivers, telling him that he is glad he will no longer have to put up with 'The blank wall. The silences. The *pretending*' (p. 209). He says that his mother was always trying to shelter him from the dangers of the outside world because of his asthma, and now Rivers is doing the same thing. Nevertheless, although he is clearly embarrassed by the gesture, he

 CHECK THE POEM

Rivers's concern about Prior's susceptibility to gas on pp. 208–9 is a reminder that chemical warfare was a frightening innovation of the Great War. Wilfred Owen describes the horror of a gas attack in 'Dulce Et Decorum Est'.

finally thanks Rivers 'for putting up with me' (p. 210), and says he will write to him.

Rivers asks for Sassoon to be sent to his office once he returns to the hospital, and Sassoon tells him why he missed his Board. Rivers cannot believe he did so merely to meet a friend. Sassoon then admits that he was not sure he wanted to face the Board. If he was passed fit, he had been planning to go to another psychiatrist for a second opinion. With two eminent doctors supporting his suitability for active service, he could not be accused of insanity if he decided to resume his protest. But he also felt that this would be betraying Rivers, so walked out in order to evade the dilemma. Rivers tells him he would have helped him get a second opinion if he had wanted it, and is extremely relieved that Sassoon is sticking to his former decision to go back to the army.

COMMENTARY

It is in this chapter that the stories of Sassoon and Prior counterbalance one another most obviously. The two characters – who never actually interact in the course of the novel – stand in direct contrast. Prior is a working-class officer who wants to return to active service but cannot, while Sassoon is an upper-class officer who is not sure he wants to return to active service, but eventually decides he will. The kind of ethical issues concerning the continuation of the war with which Sassoon is grappling never occur to Prior, for whom participation is a matter of personal pride and a means to gain social acceptance.

QUESTION

Are fatherhood and **patriarchy** portrayed as the same thing in *Regeneration*?

Prior's prickly relationship with Rivers, which has been such a significant part of the book, persists until the end. In particular, Prior retains his ability to challenge Rivers and make him, as well as the readers, think of his role in a different way. When he tells Rivers that he 'never wanted you to be *Daddy*. I'd got you lined up for a worse fate' (p. 210), he draws attention to the way in which Rivers's relationship with his patients could be regarded as as much maternal as paternal. Such an observation recalls Rivers's reflections in Chapter 9 of *Regeneration*, and it is these he presumably has in mind when he reflects that 'He was rather glad Prior didn't have access to his thoughts' (p. 210).

However, Prior's final expression of gratitude is a touching affirmation of his admiration for Rivers, however difficult he might find it to admit.

GLOSSARY

206	home service remaining in the army, but unfit for active military service overseas
206	gas cape a waterproof garment resembling a poncho that was intended to protect the wearer from the effect of gas on the skin
207	Sampson Ralph Allen Sampson (1866–1939), Astronomer Royal for Scotland
207	Polygon Wood situated near Ypres, the site of fierce fighting as part of the Battle of Passchendaele, which began on 20 September 1917
208	gas huts part of a soldier's training was to go through a hut which was flooded with gas
211	racial degeneration the idea that a race is declining mentally and physically generation by generation
212	Charles Mercier (1852–1919), psychologist and doctor who published widely on the topic of insanity

---

CHAPTER 19

- Prior sneaks into Sarah's lodgings to spend the night with her. He tells her he loves her for the first time.

- Owen and Sassoon have dinner together the night before Owen leaves Craiglockhart.

Prior climbs up to the window of Sarah's lodgings, and she lets him in. She stresses that they must keep quiet, because she is not allowed to entertain men in her room. Sarah tells Prior that she is glad that he is not going back to France, which causes him to experience a momentary flashback to the image of the eyeball resting in the palm of his hand. He realises that he will never tell her about that experience, because he values being with someone who is ignorant

QUESTION

How does Prior's decision that he will never tell Sarah about his horrific experiences in France fit in with *Regeneration*'s central theme of silence?

of the horrors of war. Yet at the same time, he wants her to know everything about him. He realises that it is a dilemma that cannot be resolved. As Sarah begins to undress him, he tells her that he loves her. She replies that she loves him too.

It is the night before Owen is due to leave Craiglockhart, and he is dining at the Conservative Club with Sassoon. Both are slightly drunk, and when Sassoon reads Owen extracts from a book of bad poetry, they find it highly amusing. Sassoon gives the book to Owen as a parting gift, along with an envelope containing a letter of introduction to Robert Ross. It is revealed that it was Sassoon who arranged Owen's early release from hospital, by going to see Rivers and persuading him that Owen has recovered from his shell-shock. Although Owen thinks it is right he should leave, as he is no longer ill, he is also reluctant to go. When Sassoon leaves, Owen sits alone in the empty room feeling an enormous sense of loss.

COMMENTARY

The two episodes that make up this chapter are linked by the theme of love. In the first, love is openly expressed, but in the other it remains undeclared. The affair between Prior and Sarah is acceptable because it is heterosexual, whereas the homosexual attraction that is hinted at between Sassoon and Owen cannot be acted upon because it is forbidden.

The scene between Prior and Sarah is full of tenderness. They have never spent a night together before, or seen each other entirely naked, and thus it is almost as if they are making love for the first time. However, the romance is undercut by the continuation of Barker's exploration of the gulf of misunderstanding that exists between men and women. When Prior looks into Sarah's eyes from very close up, 'her eyes merged into a single eye, fringed by lashes like prehistoric vegetation' (p. 215), an image that mutates into Prior's recollection of the eyeball he picked up from the floor of the trench. It is this that triggers his realisation that he will never tell her the truth about his wartime experiences, because 'if she'd known the worst parts she couldn't have gone on being a haven for him' (p. 216). Thus, Barker demonstrates that he is still making Sarah into an image that fits his desire, rather than treating her as an

CONTEXT

Writing to Sassoon on 5 November, Owen thanked him for the letter, which contained a ten-pound note as well as the letter of introduction to Robert Ross, and openly expressed his devotion: 'Know that since mid-September, when you still regarded me as a tiresome little knocker on your door, I held you as Keats + Christ + Elijah + my Colonel + my father-confessor + Amenophis IV in profile' (*Wilfred Owen: Collected Letters*, 1967, p. 505).

equal individual. Although there is no reason to think that Prior is lying when he tells Sarah he loves her, Barker strongly hints that this will be a relationship in which he will never achieve his wish 'to know and be known as deeply as possible' (p. 216).

The scene between Owen and Sassoon is equally touching, but it does not end with any kind of declaration, only a separation that leaves many things unspoken. Whenever real emotion threatens to break through, the two of them defuse it with laughter and jokes. The presence of the anonymous man in the corner reading the newspaper acts as a figure who prohibits the expression of a desire which society judges disgusting and illegal (it is significant that he only disappears when Sassoon does). Thus, the two men's period of friendship and artistic collaboration comes to an end with only a pat on the shoulder: 'Nothing else, not even "goodbye"' (p. 219). This farewell is made even more poignant if the reader is aware of its finality, since Owen was to be killed in France exactly a year later.

CONTEXT

In *The Woman's Historical Novel: British Women Writers, 1900–2000* (2005), Diana Wallace argues that the First World War 'was one of the catalysts … which made women aware of their own existence as subjects within history' (p. 220).

GLOSSARY	
214	periscope a device that allowed soldiers to look over the top of the trenches without lifting their heads above the parapet
215	camisole a form of women's undergarment that resembles a vest, and would have been worn over a corset
215	stays corset
216	sepia brown tint that typifies early photographs
217	Alymer Strong author of *A Human Voice*, published in 1917
217	Wagner Richard Wagner (1813–83), German composer
217	Brünnhilde the leading female character in Wagner's series of operas known as the Ring cycle, composed between 1848 and 1874
218	epogee variation on the term 'apogee', or the furthest or highest point

> ## CHAPTER 20
>
> - Rivers leaves Craiglockhart and moves to London to begin his new job.
> - He goes to visit the hospital where Lewis Yealland works, and accompanies him on a ward round.
> - Rivers is particularly intrigued by the case of a dumb patient who has proved resistant to any attempts to restore his speech, and asks Yealland if he can watch him being treated.

Rivers prepares to leave Craiglockhart to begin his new post at the Royal Flying Corps Hospital in London. He is pleased that Willard is walking again, although frustrated that he is still refusing to admit that his paralysis was psychological, not physical. He is also worried about Sassoon, who is continuing to write poetry, but appears to have given up hope that he can do anything to prevent the continuation of the war. Rivers feels responsible for this.

Rivers finds life in London stressful, and he begins to feel ill again. His sleep is continually disrupted by air raids, and he has a great deal of work to do. He is intrigued by his new job, though, as the experience of the Royal Flying Corps is proving his theory that shell-shock is caused by long periods of enforced inactivity rather than sudden traumatic events. He reflects that this also explains why, in peacetime, it is women who are more prone to break down.

Rivers accepts an invitation from Dr Lewis Yealland to visit his hospital. As he makes his way to his meeting with Yealland he encounters a grotesquely deformed figure crawling along the corridor. As he discovers when he joins a morning ward round, this is one of Yealland's patients, many of whom have bizarrely contracted or distorted bodies. Rivers finds Yealland himself 'impressive' (p. 224) but dictatorial, and his junior doctors are clearly nervous of his authority. He does not appear to be very sympathetic towards his patients either. He only shows interest in their physical symptoms, not their psychological state, and will not permit them to ask questions about their condition or their treatment.

One of the patients Yealland shows Rivers is a private soldier called Callan, who is dumb, and proving difficult to cure. Despite having had electrical currents applied to his throat and the ends of lighted cigarettes put on his tongue, he has not regained his voice. Yealland tells Callan that continuing to refuse to speak is not an option, and that he must recover his speech 'at once' (p. 227). Rivers asks if he can watch the procedure, and Yealland consents, providing Rivers will remain in the background. He believes that 'the last thing these patients need is a sympathetic audience' (p. 228).

CONTEXT

The case of Callan is taken from Yealland's account of his treatment of an unnamed private soldier in his book *Hysterical Disorders of Warfare*, published in 1918.

COMMENTARY

Even at the point of leaving Craiglockhart, Rivers continues to worry about his patients. His concerns regarding Willard and Sassoon remind the reader of the way in which Rivers cares about his cases as individuals and not merely as examples of symptoms. Even though Willard has been cured, Rivers remains genuinely anxious about his refusal to confront the psychological causes of his former condition. This first section of the chapter is significant because it emphasises the immense difference between Rivers's and Yealland's ideas about how shell-shock victims should be treated.

Yealland is *Regeneration*'s most unsympathetic character. Unlike Rivers, he is not an understanding, paternal figure, but represents an impersonal, 'God-like' (p. 226) authority. Although this episode is so extreme it makes Rivers 'want to laugh' (p. 224), it does not make it any less real or disturbing. The grotesquely twisted figure of the shell-shock patient whom Rivers encounters in the hospital symbolises the equally grotesque treatment regime endorsed by Yealland, in which patients are subjected to severe pain in order to force them out of their traumatised state. This individual is not depicted as human, but is described as a 'creature' (p. 223), a **point of view** which imitates Yealland's disturbingly impersonal attitude towards his patients. He is not interested in them as individuals, or concerned about how long his cure might last. Instead, he talks to them in a series of absolute statements, and shows no compassion when they exhibit signs of discomfort or fear.

CONTEXT

The term applied to the use of electrical shocks in a therapeutic context was 'faradism', after the scientist Michael Faraday (1791–1867), the discoverer of electromagnetic induction.

The introduction of Callan to the novel cannot help but call to mind the case of another hospitalised and dumb soldier – Billy Prior. Indeed, it is important for the reader to realise that if Prior had not been an officer, he would not have been sent to Rivers, but to someone like Yealland. The similarity between Callan and Prior includes more than just their symptoms: Callan's 'air of brooding antagonism' (p. 226) suggests that he has the same insubordinate and stubbornly uncooperative nature we have already witnessed in Prior. But unlike Rivers, whose treatment of Prior has involved a long process of negotiation and persuasion, Yealland merely tells Callan that he will get better, indicating his extreme confidence in his own techniques.

GLOSSARY

223	National Hospital	National Hospital for the Paralysed and Epileptic at Queen's Square in London
224	malevolent	spiteful
225	hemianalgesia	loss of sensitivity to pain on one side of the body
225	lumbar region	lower part of the spine

CHAPTER 21

- Rivers watches Callan's treatment.
- Yealland locks Callan in the room, and does not permit him to leave until he speaks.

Rivers and Yealland go to the electrical treatment room, and Yealland pulls down the blinds, leaving most of the room in darkness. When Callan comes in, Yealland locks the door, telling him that he will not be allowed to leave until he can speak. He then restrains Callan in a chair and applies electrical shocks to his throat for an hour before Callan is able to utter a sound. Yealland continues to shock Callan until he can repeat the letters of the alphabet. Exhausted, Callan runs to the door in an attempt to escape, but cannot. Rivers finds witnessing the procedure a strain, particularly when the sounds Callan makes remind him of his own stammer.

Even when Callan regains some use of his voice, Yealland carries on with the treatment, denying him water or rest. When he threatens to increase the strength of the current, Callan begins to recite the days of the week. Eventually Yealland decides Callan has been cured and asks him if he is pleased, but is annoyed when Callan only smiles in response. In order to ensure that he does not do so again, Yealland applies an electrode to the side of Callan's mouth. He is not satisfied until Callan, unsmiling, salutes and formally thanks him.

COMMENTARY

This scene is one of the most disturbing in *Regeneration*. Yealland's methods resemble torture more than treatment – he deprives Callan of his freedom and causes him extreme pain until he does what Yealland wants. His display of locking the door and 'ostentatiously dropping the key into his top pocket' (p. 229) illustrates his supreme confidence that his treatment will work, for – as Rivers realises – he is effectively imprisoning himself as well as Callan.

Rivers's reaction to what he witnesses makes it obvious that his sympathy lies with the patient, not his fellow doctor. His strong feelings of 'empathy' (p. 230) cause him to almost physically mimic Callan: he remains immobile because Callan does not move, and when Callan struggles to speak, Rivers has 'to stop himself trying to make the sound for him' (p. 231).

The final humiliation for Callan is that he is required to use his newly regained voice to thank Yealland. Unlike Rivers, who encourages his patients to converse with him as an essential part of his therapeutic process, Yealland is not interested in listening to the men he treats. The only words he will hear are those he has instructed them to say, which is a final assertion of his power. For further discussion of Yealland's treatment of Callan, see **Extended commentaries – Text 3**.

> **CONTEXT**
>
> Although Barker's portrayal of Yealland is extremely negative, in *No Man's Land: Combat and Identity in World War 1* (1979), Eric Leed stresses that 'Yealland's administration of the disciplinary therapy was not unusual, nor did he consider it unnecessarily cruel … The electrical apparatus was merely an instrument that tested the fixity of the symptom' (p. 175).

GLOSSARY

229	ostentatiously flamboyantly
229	pharyngeal referring to the throat, or pharynx
232	Mons the first battle fought by the British Army against the Germans, on 23 August 1914. Yealland is aiming to remind Callan that he is a professional soldier, who has participated in the war from the beginning
232	expiratory breathing out

CONTEXT

Barker's frequent descriptions of Rivers's dreams have an important function. Rivers suffered from an unusual impediment, which was a lack of visual memory; as Barker herself says, 'except in dreams or when he was suffering a feverish illness, he had no memory at all' ('With the Listener in Mind', *Critical Perspectives on Pat Barker*, 2005, p. 176). It is for this reason that Barker conveys a great deal of information about Rivers's reaction to past events through references to his dreams.

CHAPTER 22

- Rivers is exhausted after his visit to Yealland, and continues to feel ill.
- He has a nightmare in which he is inserting a bit into a man's mouth.
- Upon waking, he analyses the dream as indicating that he and Yealland are both in the business of silencing war protest.
- Rivers comes to acknowledge that he is directly responsible for persuading Sassoon to give up his Declaration.

After his visit to Yealland, Rivers attempts to continue work on his paper for the Royal Society, but gives up as he is feeling ill and exhausted. In an attempt to settle himself, he goes for a walk, then returns to his rooms to sleep.

Rivers then experiences a vivid nightmare which is set in Yealland's hospital. He sees again the deformed man he encountered in the corridor, who recites the opening lines of Sassoon's Declaration to him. He then finds himself in the electrical treatment room trying to force a horse's bit into the mouth of a resisting patient. He awakes with a cry.

Rivers realises that the dream has arisen directly from the events of his stressful day. Although he and Yealland were consistently courteous towards each other, he realises that it was a confrontational meeting, demonstrated by the fact that his stammer has worsened. He attempts to work out what the dream's deeper meaning might be. He wonders if the second patient might represent Prior, since he is aware of the similarities between Prior and Callan. He recalls the 'momentary spasm of satisfaction' (p. 237) that he experienced when he probed Prior's throat with the teaspoon in the course of his initial examination, but he also knows that he inflicted far less pain on Prior than Yealland did on Callan.

However, he then thinks that the 'dream seemed to be saying, in dream language, don't flatter yourself. There *is* no distinction' (p. 238). Both Rivers and Yealland share the same job, which is to silence their patients' protests and return them to the war. In that context, when Yealland forces Callan to speak he is actually, paradoxically, silencing him – which is exactly what Rivers himself is doing.

But for Rivers this is not the whole answer, which is much more specific. The patient in the chair, he finally realises, is neither Callan nor Prior, but Sassoon. As dawn breaks, Rivers is forced to admit to himself that he is to blame for Sassoon's decision to give up his protest.

COMMENTARY

It is in this chapter that Rivers surrenders his belief that he and Yealland are different. When he witnessed Callan's treatment, he clearly identified more with the patient than the therapist, but his dream tells him that he cannot make this distinction between Yealland's brutal methods and his own, even if his are 'infinitely more gentle' (p. 238). In the final analysis, both of them are part of a system in whose interests they have no choice but to act.

Rivers's reflections on his dream evoke the novel's ongoing concern with speech and silence, and draw the readers' attention to a central paradox. In making Callan speak, Yealland is actually silencing him, since Callan's dumbness is an eloquent protest against the horrors he has both witnessed and participated in. Once he can speak, he can be reabsorbed into the military machine. Likewise, Rivers may

CONTEXT

'Scold's bridle' (p. 238) is the term used to describe a locking iron headpiece which fixed a metal rod in the subject's mouth in order to prevent him or her from speaking. The name derives from its use as a punishment for women thought to be loud and abusive.

CHECK THE BOOK

Fredric Manning's *Her Privates We* (1930) is a fictionalised account of the author's experience of serving on the Somme in Western France. One of its main themes is the way in which the war encourages the development of close, caring relationships between men.

think he 'cures' his own patients, but he may be ignoring what their symptoms are trying to say.

Although Rivers doesn't think the dream can be interpreted in this general way, in the context of the novel, it does make sense. Yet his final belief that the dream is specifically about Sassoon is also valid, since it illustrates both the depth of Rivers's attachment to Sassoon and the extent of his betrayal. However kindly and however well-intentioned he might have been, he is directly responsible for persuading Sassoon to give up his pacifist views. Thus, however hard Rivers tries to persuade himself otherwise, he cannot avoid the conclusion that he has been as effective as Yealland in the silencing of antiwar protest.

GLOSSARY

235	Adam naming created things in Genesis, God creates the first man, Adam, who then names all other living things
236	horse's bit part of the bridle, a metal bar placed in a horse's mouth in order to control its speed, direction and movements
238	recalcitrant defiant, obstinate

CHAPTER 23

- Rivers tells Head about his nightmare and his conclusions regarding its meaning. Head reassures him that he is not as guilty as he thinks.

- Rivers feels that, with the help of his patients, his own healing has begun.

- Sassoon goes before the Medical Board, and is passed fit to return to duty.

- Rivers writes the formal discharge note, despite his continuing worries that Sassoon is seeking to die in battle.

Rivers is sitting in Head's room, having told him about his nightmare and what he thinks it means. Head does not agree with his conclusions. Instead, he assures Rivers that nothing he has done has forced Sassoon to give up his protest. He argues that Sassoon's strong sense of integrity means that his return to the war was always inevitable, because he would never stay in hospital unnecessarily. He is also of the opinion that Rivers's idea that he and Yealland are the same is nonsense, arguing that he 'can't imagine anybody less like Yealland – methods, attitudes, values – everything' (p. 240). Rivers is reassured, but says that he remains worried about Sassoon, whom he thinks is returning to the front with the aim of getting killed.

The two men begin to talk about Ruth's belief that Rivers has changed a great deal. Rivers says that he has had the chance to change before, but did not act on it, recalling a research trip to the Solomon Islands when he realised that all his beliefs meant nothing to the islanders. It brought him a sense 'of the most *amazing* freedom' (p. 242) because he suddenly understood that the standards that govern his life are not absolute. He thinks that his experiences at Craiglockhart have brought him to this realisation again, continuing the process of healing 'even if not in the expected direction' (p. 242).

CHECK THE BOOK
Barker depicts Rivers's trip to the Solomon Islands and the effect that it had upon him in a series of **flashbacks** in *The Ghost Road*.

Rivers then returns to Craiglockhart for a final time in order to attend Sassoon's Board. Sassoon tells him that he has finished his book of poems, and promises to give him the first copy.

Sassoon's Board goes well, as his attitude and his distinguished war record impresses the Medical Officers. Unexpectedly, however, Sassoon maintains his belief in his Declaration, saying that not only has he not changed his mind, but he has become even more strongly convinced that his views are correct. Nevertheless, he also firmly believes that it is his duty to go back to the army.

Rivers and Sassoon say goodbye as Sassoon prepares to leave Craiglockhart following the successful conclusion of his Board. He is clearly very anxious to go, and keenly anticipating his return to France. In the entrance hall, he comes to attention and salutes

Rivers, thanks him and departs; actions that briefly remind Rivers of the conclusion to Callan's treatment.

Rivers sits down at his desk to deal with the paperwork from the Board, and recognises the irony that Sassoon does not even realise the part he has played in changing Rivers. Rivers remembers how his first attempt to change his life failed, and wonders why he has succeeded now. He thinks that it is because it has happened without him being aware, and that all his patients have played a part in the process. He has gone from holding extremely conservative views to being in disagreement with the authorities 'over a very wide range of issues' (p. 249), and hopes that his middle-aged rebellion might be able to succeed where the rebellion of the young has not.

Nevertheless, Rivers remains worried about Sassoon. He believes that Sassoon hates the war as much as ever, and that the sense of honour that compelled him to return to France will not survive the brutal realities of warfare. Death, he fears, might be the only way to resolve such a dilemma. When Rivers comes to Sassoon's file, however, he has no other choice but to formally record Sassoon's discharge from Craiglockhart.

COMMENTARY

A superficial reading of this chapter might conclude that it rounds *Regeneration* off very satisfactorily. Rivers is reassured by Head that he does not resemble Yealland and is not responsible for Sassoon's decision to return to the front. Furthermore, Rivers feels that he has been fundamentally altered by his experiences at Craiglockhart, and sees it as a chance to reject his 'reticent, introverted, reclusive' life (p. 249) in order to become a more active agent for change. Sassoon, too, gets what he wanted – the chance to return to active service without actually disowning the views expressed in his Declaration.

We should never forget, however, that Barker has focused her narration throughout through the viewpoints of specific characters, which means that the text lacks the trustworthiness implied by the use of an omniscient, detached, third-person narrator. Throughout the chapter, Barker hints that Rivers's optimism about the future may not be entirely justified. His experience in the Solomon Islands has already given him an awareness that his white, educated and masculine viewpoint is not unalterable or unchallengeable, and we have seen his opinions about the war change under the influence of patients such as Sassoon and Prior. However, it remains unclear what difference such realisations will actually make to Rivers's life.

It is Rivers's continuing worries about Sassoon, in particular, that undercut his renewed sense of hope. In the brief insights we are given into his state of mind, Sassoon regards his future in a characteristically uncomplicated way, experiencing 'No doubts, no scruples, no agonizing, just a straightforward, headlong retreat towards the front' (p. 248). Yet the paradoxical idea of a 'retreat towards the front' – which is more normally retreated *from* – indicates that Sassoon's return to active service may in fact be enabling him to evade the ethical complexities he has been grappling with ever since he began his protest. Similarly, his refusal to talk about his continuing nightmares also suggests that the issues that brought Sassoon to Craiglockhart might not actually have been resolved at all.

The other members of the Board, who do not know Sassoon as Rivers does, are easily impressed by his reputation and his robust appearance and see no problem in releasing him from hospital. Only Rivers remains concerned that Sassoon will not be able to serve as a soldier and maintain his allegiance to his pacifist views, and that the tension between the two positions is leading him to develop 'a genuine and very deep desire for death' (p. 250). But in spite of his misgivings, Rivers's final act in the novel is to fill in the last page of Sassoon's file with the words '*Nov. 26, 1917. Discharged to duty*' (p. 250). His conclusion that there 'was nothing more he wanted to say that he could say' (p. 250) implies that Rivers has been silenced as effectively as any of the soldiers he has treated. There is simply no language he can use in a clinical context with which to express his doubts, which leaves him with no option but to use the only words that the authorities will recognise. Yet the awareness underlying that act is that writing them may well place Rivers back in the very role of father–murderer that he is attempting to disown.

CONTEXT

Sassoon did not return to the trenches of the Western Front immediately, nor was he to die in action as Rivers feared. In February 1918, he was posted to Palestine, and did not arrive back in France until May. On 13 July, he made a foolhardy foray into No Man's Land in order to locate a German machine-gun post, and was shot in the head by one of his own men. He was sent home to England for treatment on 18 July, and Rivers visited him in hospital. Barker recreates this part of Sassoon's history in *The Eye in the Door*.

? **QUESTION**

Do you regard
Sassoon's return to
the front line as a
necessity, or do
you agree with
Elaine Showalter's
opinion that
Sassoon's 'therapy
was a seduction
and a negotiation;
his return to
France, an
acknowledgement
of defeat' (*The
Female Malady*,
1985, p. 187)?

GLOSSARY

241	self-deprecating modest
241	guinea a coin worth twenty-one shillings
241	kinship structure the social organisation of family and marriage
243	haemophobia fear of blood
244–5	mildew and blackspot common diseases afflicting roses
245	DSO Distinguished Service Order; a military award given to officers
247	eugenics a belief that human evolution should be aided by human intervention, such as selective breeding
249	reticent uncommunicative, unwilling to speak

EXTENDED COMMENTARIES

TEXT 1 – CHAPTER 5, PAGES 45–8

From 'Shortly before dawn he woke …' to '… bristles, near-boiling water and pins.'

This passage details a vivid dream experienced by Rivers, and his attempts to analyse its meaning. As with much of *Regeneration*, it is based on an actual event – the experiments the real Rivers carried out with his colleague Henry Head between 1903 and 1907 into the regeneration of nerves. A surgeon cut two nerves in Head's forearm then stitched the ends together again, and for the following five years Head and Rivers charted the healing process.

It is through Rivers's analysis of the dream and the memories that it evokes that the meaning of the title of the novel is explained. Until this point, *Regeneration* does not seem a particularly appropriate title for a narrative about acutely traumatised soldiers such as Burns who seem to be incurable. The *Oxford English Dictionary*'s definition of 'regeneration' is 'bring or come into a renewed existence', which would seem to be an impossibility for most of Rivers's patients. Through her portrayal of Rivers's dream, however, Barker is able to demonstrate that the process of renewal is a long and complicated one that will inevitably involve pain. The Head–Rivers experiment, even though it happens long before the events in the novel begin, becomes the central symbol for the process endured by most of its characters.

The other significance of this passage is that it marks the point in the novel where Rivers himself begins to be drawn into the regenerative process. At the beginning of his dream he is occupying the same position he did in the actual experiment: that of detached observer. But this begins to be compromised almost immediately by the distress he feels on causing Head pain, which makes him strongly desire to stop the experiment. Rivers himself then becomes the subject of the experiment when his own arm is cut by Head, and it is this in particular that causes him to reflect on the extent to which 'he was already experimenting on himself' (p. 48).

Just as Head has to suffer pain as a necessary part of the process of healing, so 'the mental lives of Rivers's patients must be stripped down, and exposed to the rawness of their emotions, in order to rebuild themselves' (John Brannigan, *Pat Barker*, 2005, p. 98). But, as Brannigan also argues, encouraging men to express their emotions contradicts everything society has taught them about being a 'proper' man, since '[m]anliness is about repressing emotions' (*Pat Barker*, p. 98). Rivers feels sympathy for his patients, and this means that he has to battle with his own feelings even as he encourages the men he treats to express theirs. Analysing the dream, he recognises the **irony** that 'In advising his young patients to abandon the attempt at repression and to let themselves *feel* the pity and terror their war experience inevitably evoked, he was excavating the ground he stood on' (p. 48). Thus, Barker draws her readers' attention to the fact that Rivers is being forced to redefine his own beliefs in the course of treating others.

Rivers is placed in rather a strange position in this episode: that of analysing himself. He is a skilled interpreter of other people's dreams – but is he as competent when trying to read his own? The passage shows him running through a number of different possible meanings – the Freudian view 'that all dreams were wish fulfilment' (p. 46), the idea that it could represent his own feelings of conflict

CONTEXT

Sigmund Freud writes in *The Interpretation of Dreams* (1899): 'That all the material composing the content of a dream is somehow derived from experience, that it is reproduced or remembered in the dream – this at least may be accepted as an incontestable fact. Yet it would be wrong to assume that such a connection between the dream-content and reality will be easily obvious from a comparison between the two. On the contrary, the connection must be carefully sought, and in quite a number of cases it may for a long while elude discovery'.

about the continuation of the war, and the extent to which his treatment challenges his own habit of emotional repression. Although by the end of the chapter, Rivers has arrived at a satisfactory interpretation, Barker hints that he may have evaded some of the most uncomfortable implications of his dream. When he considers, for example, that it might have a sexual meaning, he decides that it's an interpretation he 'couldn't accept' (p. 47), and moves on. He then reflects that he had been 'thinking about Sassoon immediately before he went to sleep', and wonders whether he is becoming influenced by Sassoon's antiwar stance – but again, it is something he refuses to think about, concluding that he 'couldn't see that the dream was a likely dramatization of that conflict' (p. 47).

With these two very noticeable avoidances – Rivers's refusal to 'accept' and to 'see' – Barker is inviting us to adopt an ironic distance from her character. Sassoon's biographer Jean Moorcroft Wilson claims that Rivers was 'almost certainly homosexual by inclination' (*Siegfried Sassoon: The Making of a War Poet*, 1998, p. 393), and Barker suggests the same thing at other points in *Regeneration*. Thus, while Rivers does appear to learn something about himself during his session of self-analysis, he has also dodged any implications his dream might have regarding his sexuality.

TEXT 2 – CHAPTER 8, PAGES 82–5

From 'Sassoon reached the last book ...' to '... Yes, I will. Thank you.'

This conversation between Wilfred Owen and Siegfried Sassoon during their first meeting becomes very profound very quickly when they begin to discuss how the war can be represented in poetry, which may never be quite able to convey the experience of the soldier on the front line. When Owen compliments Sassoon on his poem 'The Redeemer', he draws attention to Sassoon's use of Christian imagery in his comparison between a soldier carrying planks and Christ carrying his cross. Yet Sassoon is rather self-critical, arguing not only that it is an easy comparison to make, but that it is also one that doesn't quite work, since 'Christ isn't on record as having lobbed many Mills bombs' (p. 82).

CHECK THE BOOK
Barker returns to the question of the role of art in a time of war in her 2007 novel, *Life Class*, which is also set during the First World War.

This raises the unsettling thought that the war may lie beyond any existing system of morality or representation. Both Owen and Sassoon have experienced moments when they have been confronted with a sense that it is something exceptionally profound and horrifying: in Owen's words, 'as if all other wars had somehow … distilled themselves into this war, and that makes it something you … almost can't challenge' (p. 83). The hesitancy of his speech here suggests both how difficult it is to talk about war without resorting to comfortable symbols, and his determination to do so. And if Owen thinks of the war as something that extends back into the past, Sassoon describes it as reaching forward into the future, claiming that 'A hundred years from now they'll still be ploughing up skulls' (p. 84). From our perspective, we know that he is right; and this has the effect of drawing us into the First World War and making us part of its continuing story.

The implications of their conversation are deeply chilling: that war is an inescapable condition of human existence. The trenches look as if they 'had always been there' (p. 83), and skulls appear to sprout out of their walls like 'mushrooms' (p. 83). For a moment, the conflict has been moved out of the realm of history and time and become something primitive and primeval – the expression of a tendency to violence that makes a mockery of any twentieth-century concepts of 'civilisation' or 'progress'. Both men recognise this – it makes 'the nape of Sassoon's neck' crawl (p. 83) – and fall silent, because 'They'd gone further than either of them had intended, and for a moment they didn't know how to get back' (p. 84). Yet the perceptive reader will realise that, while silence may be an absolutely appropriate response to such horror, Sassoon and Owen's inability to speak at this moment is also ironic. The reason for their appearance in Barker's work – the very reason we still recognise their names today – is their eloquent and innovative verse directly depicting the suffering of warfare.

Through Owen and Sassoon, Barker is contemplating what *Regeneration* itself represents; an extension of the project they themselves began in their attempt to make their experience of the trenches into art. Owen's admission to Sassoon that he has not yet written about the war because he thinks poetry should be 'the

CHECK THE NET
In an article published in the *Daily Telegraph* in January 2008 describing a tour of the French battlefields, the journalist Nigel Richardson observes that 'Still today bodies are unearthed at an average of five a year' ('Battlefield Tours: Behind the Lines'). Go to **www.telegraph. co.uk**, type 'battlefield tours Richardson' into the search box on the home page and follow the link.

opposite of all that. The ugliness' (p. 84) is amusing to a modern audience because his name is now synonymous with the First World War, but it also raises more serious questions regarding the function of literature in the context of conflict. Should it be used to force us to confront the 'ugliness' of war, or should it reassure us, reinforcing moral certainties and reminding us of better times? The answer, clearly, is that, as the poetry of Owen and Sassoon demonstrates, the attempt must be made to represent war in art. In this way, the audience will be helped 'to have "sufficient imagination" to realize the horror of war in order to prevent its continuation or recurrence' (Karin Westman, *Pat Barker's Regeneration*, 2001, p. 56).

TEXT 3 – CHAPTER 21, PAGES 229–33

From 'I am going to lock the door ...' to '... Thank you, sir.'

The emphasis in this passage is on speech, and particularly the paradox of being forced to speak, but not being listened to. Yealland talks to Callan throughout in a series of absolute and unambiguous statements: 'I am going to lock the door' (p. 229); 'You cannot leave the room' (p. 231); 'You must utter a sound' (p. 232). He asks questions of his patient very rarely, and when he does, there is only one answer he is prepared to hear. A good example of this is when he asks Callan, 'Are you not pleased to be cured?' When Callan only smiles, he is electrocuted again until he is prepared to give the correct response: 'Thank you, sir' (p. 233).

Yealland's function is to bring the disciplinary aspect of the therapist's role to the forefront of the text. As the critic Elaine Showalter says, 'his blatant use of power and authority was part of the therapy' (*The Female Malady*, 1985, p. 177). The historian Eric Leed observes that this kind of disciplinary treatment based itself deliberately upon the 'principle and techniques derived from animal training' (*No Man's Land*, 1979, p. 173), such as the use of pain and isolation in order to compel obedience; and we might indeed think that Callan is not being treated like a human being. All that is important to Yealland is that Callan obeys him; he is not at all interested in engaging him in a conversation once he has recovered his voice. As he says at one point in the treatment process, 'with

QUESTION

What is the relationship between speech and silence in *Regeneration*?

great emphasis: "*You must speak, but I will not listen to anything you have to say*'" (p. 231).

As well as employing pain, Yealland's other tactic is to remind Callan of the heroic identity that his dumbness has taken away, telling him to 'Remember you must behave as becomes the hero I expect you to be' (p. 230). His mention of Callan's involvement in the Battle of Mons, the first British engagement of the First World War, highlights the fact that Callan has been fighting since 1914, and identifies him as a professional soldier rather than a volunteer or a conscript. If even hardened soldiers like Callan can break down, then nobody is immune, and this makes his silence an even more eloquent protest than most. Callan's case thus highlights the importance of 'curing' shell-shocked individuals, who must not be permitted to disrupt the masculine, heroic codes that impel men to endure the suffering of warfare.

Yealland himself, although not a soldier, upholds these same beliefs, and this is shown in the way in which he makes the therapy session a battle of wills. When he 'ostentatiously' (p. 229) locks the door, he makes sure that Callan sees him, and, as Rivers observes, this means that 'There could be no backing down' (p. 229). So even when Callan resumes his properly 'manly' identity, Yealland emphasises his own superior masculinity, because he retains ultimate power and authority.

The **narrative point of view** in this passage is particularly interesting. Barker does not give us access to Yealland's mind at any point, so we always view him from Rivers's perspective. The reader is fleetingly reminded of Rivers's presence in the room at moments when he has a particularly strong reaction to something that he sees, but for the most part he remains in the background. Thus it is easy to forget that the Yealland who appears in *Regeneration* is not an unbiased portrait, but always coloured by Rivers's reaction against a treatment regime so unlike his own. We are certainly not meant to sympathise with Yealland and his brutal methods, but his real significance is to act as a focus for Rivers's meditations on his own role.

CONTEXT

The British Expeditionary Force, or BEF, was made up of Britain's professional, or 'standing', army, and entered the war in 1914. The New Army, or 'Kitchener's Army', was formed from volunteers who came forward in response to the recruitment drive launched in 1914, but because they had to be trained, these men did not begin active duty in France until 1915.

PART THREE

CRITICAL APPROACHES

CHARACTERISATION

W. H. R. RIVERS

Rivers is undoubtedly the central character in *Regeneration*. Not only does the story keep returning to descriptions of his experiences and emotions, he also plays an important unifying function within the novel. *Regeneration* features a wide-ranging group of characters, many of whom never interact with each other in the course of the narrative. Sassoon, for example, does not know Billy Prior, and Henry Head never meets any of the patients at Craiglockhart. Rivers is the only connection between these individuals, and only a few relationships develop outside of his sphere of influence. Billy Prior's relationship with Sarah Lumb, and Owen and Sassoon's poetic collaboration both take place independently of him, but these are rare examples. For the most part, Rivers is the figure around whom all of the other characters revolve.

He is also the most mobile character in *Regeneration*. His period of leave in the second half of the novel provides a welcome relief from the often claustrophobic setting of Craiglockhart, introducing the reader to different characters and other places apart from the hospital and its surrounding area. Nor does Barker allow us to forget that before the war Rivers was an anthropologist, whose research took him to exotic locations that few other Europeans in the late nineteenth and early twentieth centuries would have seen. At several points in the novel he refers to his experiences in Melanesia, and it is obvious that they have greatly influenced him. This counterbalances the fact that Rivers, who has an honorary military rank, and whose job is to treat soldiers, has not been to the Western Front, nor had any direct experience of warfare.

But although he acts as the glue that holds the novel together, Rivers is not exempt from the dilemmas around which the narrative centres, such as the conflict between patriotic duty and personal

CONTEXT

In her study *Pat Barker* (2002), Sharon Monteith warns that 'the consequences of including a historical figure in a fiction can sometimes be the limitation of the fiction. It is a mistake simply to correlate the facts we glean about Rivers with the fiction in the way some critics reduce the work to fit the facts' (p. 70).

CONTEXT

Rivers had the rank of Captain in the Royal Army Medical Corps, or RAMC.

honour, and its presentation of masculinity in crisis. One of the main preoccupations of *Regeneration* is the tracing of Rivers's altering attitude towards the war. He begins the novel believing that it 'must be fought to a finish, for the sake of the succeeding generations' (p. 47), but as he continues to witness the war's terrible effect upon the minds and bodies of the men who fight it, his view changes. Two of his patients play a particularly important part in this process, although in different ways. First, David Burns acts as a graphic representation of a life ruined beyond all Rivers's attempts to repair it. All Rivers can do is watch Burns suffer and sympathise helplessly with the horror of his condition. Second, Siegfried Sassoon engages Rivers in rational debate about the morality of allowing the conflict to continue. Although Rivers is meant to be persuading Sassoon to give up his antiwar protest – a task in which he succeeds – Sassoon's arguments nevertheless make increasing sense to him, causing him to reflect upon 'how much easier his life would have been if they'd sent Siegfried somewhere else' (p. 115). By the end of *Regeneration*, Rivers condemns himself for silencing his patients; fitting 'young men back into the role of warrior, a role they had – however unconsciously – rejected' (p. 238).

Rivers often adopts the role of father-figure to the men under his care, and examples of his compassion are numerous. Throughout *Regeneration* he is shown putting his patients' concerns before his own, exhausting himself to the point of physical breakdown. But his fatherly persona is itself rather problematic, because Rivers himself is the main character through whom the role of the father is criticised. This is highlighted through Barker's description of Rivers's relationship with his own father, a very strict authority figure. Rivers's persistent stammer, which he has had all his life, comes to represent his own rebellion against his father who, as a speech therapist, has been unsuccessful in his attempts to 'cure' his son. Thus, Rivers is both a rebellious son and a father who, however reluctantly, compels obedience from others, which is an uncomfortable combination. The tension between the two roles is maintained right up to the end of the novel, when Rivers certifies Sassoon fit to return to active service. Although he has come to see himself as rebelling against the military machine, forced 'into conflict with the authorities over a very wide range of issues'

> **CONTEXT**
>
> In his essay 'War Stories', Blake Morrison credits Barker with rescuing Rivers from his obscure position 'only as a footnote in the history of the Great War' (*New Yorker*, January 1996, p. 78).

(p. 249), he nevertheless writes the final report that confirms he has done his job and brought Sassoon's public antiwar protest to an end.

Rivers's growing friendship with Sassoon is a central aspect of *Regeneration*, not only because of the part it plays in changing his opinions regarding the war, but also because it enables Barker to hint at Rivers's sexual orientation, thus linking him to the novel's interest in the portrayal of homosexuality. Rivers appears to be a rather sexless figure – he has never married, and no significant relationships with any women are mentioned. However, his tolerant attitude towards homosexuality in his patients is unusual for the time. He reacts sympathetically when Sassoon confesses his own homosexuality, and is even able to joke with him about it.

Barker's portrayal of Rivers is overwhelmingly positive. He is insightful, kind, humorous and surprisingly open-minded – although his encounters with the working-class officer Billy Prior reveal that his prejudices regarding social class are rather deeply ingrained. But even his inconsistencies are dealt with sympathetically, encouraging us to see him as an essentially good man caught up in the dilemmas caused by a difficult period in history.

SIEGFRIED SASSOON

Of all the characters in *Regeneration*, it is Siegfried Sassoon who conforms most easily to the conventional role of hero. Barker makes several references to his height and good looks, which is unusual in a novel that is more concerned with internal states than external appearance. On his train journey to Craiglockhart at the very beginning of the book, we are told that he attracts 'Admiring glances' from his fellow travellers – 'and not only from the women' (p. 5) – and at his final Medical Board one officer is openly impressed by his 'physique' (p. 247). Upper class and well connected, Sassoon is also highly intelligent and honourable; the very attributes that have led him to embark upon his controversial antiwar protest.

But although Sassoon appears to be, and in many ways is, an exemplary soldier-poet, he is as flawed and contradictory as any

The notion that the historical Rivers was attracted to Sassoon on a personal level has been supported by Barker. In an interview she gave on the publication of *Regeneration*'s sequel, *The Eye in the Door*, she said, 'I do suspect Rivers was in love with him. There's quite a lot of indirect evidence' (Candice Rodd, 'A Stomach for War', *Independent on Sunday*, 12 September 1993).

other figure in *Regeneration*. His German first name and Jewish family name compromise his status as an officer and a gentleman, just as his Declaration is a surprising departure from his previously unblemished military record. While there is no doubt that Sassoon embarks upon his protest with the best of intentions, he has little grasp of the intricacies of his situation. He may be an eloquent poet, but Barker does not portray him as a particularly deep thinker. Rivers regards Sassoon as a man who has 'so many good qualities', while also possessing a 'self-absorption' that is 'remarkable' (p. 116).

This is also evident in Sassoon's attitude towards his homosexuality. His honesty regarding his sexual orientation is admirable: he refuses to copy the example of his friend Robert Ross, who opposes the war in private in order to evade the attention of the authorities. While he may never actually name himself as a homosexual, he frankly admits to Rivers that it was not until he read Edward Carpenter's book *The Intermediate Sex* that he realised he 'wasn't just a freak' who 'didn't seem able to feel … well. Any of the things you were supposed to feel' (p. 54). Consequently, he refuses to hide his friendships with men such as Ross, arguing that just because 'I *can't* conform in one area of life' it doesn't mean that 'I *have* to conform in the others' (p. 205). Rivers, though, is frustrated that Sassoon cannot see the risks he runs in making himself such a controversial figure, and argues that it may damage others as well as himself: 'You spend far too much time tilting at windmills, Siegfried. In ways which do *you* a great deal of damage … and don't do anybody else any good at all' (p. 205).

Towards the end of the novel, the **narrative point of view** withdraws from Sassoon. This leaves the reader with little way to judge the accuracy of Rivers's impression that Sassoon's decision to return to active service – while still retaining his belief that the war is immoral – will deepen rather than resolve his dilemmas. It is, however, clear that Sassoon, ever the man of action rather than reflection, regards the battlefield as a place where he can escape the complexities of his situation: 'No doubt, no scruples, no agonizing, just a straightforward, headlong retreat towards the front' (p. 248).

> **CONTEXT**
>
> The Sassoons were a prosperous Jewish merchant family from Iraq; Siegfried's great-grandfather, David Sassoon, settled in England in 1858.

> **CONTEXT**
>
> The phrase 'headlong retreat towards the front', though used here to describe Sassoon, is actually taken from one of Wilfred Owen's final letters to him. While stationed in a base camp in Étaples in 1918 and waiting to return to the trenches, he wrote 'Everything is clear now; and I am in hasty retreat towards the Front'.

BILLY PRIOR

Billy Prior is the only principal male character in the novel who is entirely fictional, and he provides an important point of contrast to the other masculine figures in the book. Barker herself has indicated that his real significance is 'to bring out certain facets of Rivers's character that I couldn't bring out through Sassoon or any of the others. I needed someone basically to be fairly antagonistic to Rivers' (quoted in Donna Perry, *Backtalk: Women Writers Speak Out*, 1993, pp. 52–3). Prior is never depicted as interacting with any other character at Craiglockhart but Rivers, and the conversations between them are consistently tense and combative. Prior delights in shocking Rivers and his resistance to authority and his constant questioning often make Rivers uneasy. It is a testimony to his skill as a therapist that Prior is successfully cured of the amnesia that is the main symptom of his war trauma, even though his return to active service is prohibited due to his worsening asthma.

Prior's combative attitude is shown to originate from his awareness that he is an outsider in the world of Craiglockhart because of his origins. He is an army officer, but unlike the other patients he is not upper or middle class. Instead, he is what was known as a 'temporary gentleman': someone from a lower-class background who has been promoted to officer rank. Prior is suffering from dumbness when he is first admitted to Craiglockhart, but once he recovers the power of speech the first thing Rivers notices about his voice is his northern accent, 'not ungrammatical, but with the vowel sounds distinctly flattened' (p. 49). For Rivers, this has 'the curious effect of making him *look* different. Thinner, more defensive. And, at the same time, a lot tougher' (p. 49). This both accentuates Rivers's own class prejudice and reminds the reader that Prior's position is an oddity. Barker argues that this makes him the character with whom the reader of *Regeneration* can most easily identify: 'His perspective is our perspective because it's the perspective of the outsider – in class, in sexuality and in temperament' (quoted in Mark Sinker, 'Temporary Gentlemen', 1997, *Sight and Sound*, p. 24).

Rivers's conversations with both Prior's parents reveal that, handicapped by his asthma, he has had to struggle for everything

CHECK THE FILM

In the 1997 film adaptation of *Regeneration* the part of Billy Prior is played by Jonny Lee Miller with a northeast accent, although in the *Regeneration* trilogy Prior is depicted as originating from Salford, near Manchester.

that he has gained in life. In addition, his mother's desire that he 'better' himself had led to him becoming alienated from his class background even before the war. Due to her influence he has become stranded across the class divide, and it is something that he cannot quite forgive her for. As Prior admits in his final conversation with Rivers before he leaves Craiglockhart, he has transferred his hostility onto Rivers, who not only represents the system that will always regard him as different, but takes on his mother's role of the figure who keeps him in his position as outsider. As we learn in Chapter 6, Prior's mother felt that her asthmatic son should be protected from the hardships of working-class life, and he comes to regard Rivers's decision that his asthma precludes him from returning to the front as similarly prohibiting him from joining in with the rough-and-tumble of a masculine community. For Prior, active war service is the way to prove his own resilience and to gain a social acceptance not otherwise available to him, and he bitterly resents being prevented from returning to the front line.

Prior is also distinctive in being the only male figure in the novel who has an active, heterosexual, sex life. His relationship with Sarah Lumb, which begins as a casual affair, and ends with a mutual declaration of love, is unique in a world populated by characters who experience deep anxieties about their sexuality, and who consequently feel themselves to be emasculated and therefore powerless. Prior, in contrast, has no problems finding sex freely available wherever he wants it: as he says to Rivers, '*I don't pay*' (p. 67). Unlike Rivers's other patients, for whom the topic is a deep and genuine concern, Prior can joke about sexuality, and makes frequent use of sexual innuendo in his consultation sessions. He does so out of a juvenile desire to shock, but also to evade deeper anxieties about his war experiences. Asked about how he felt on going into combat, he retorts that it reminded him of 'those men who lurk around in bushes waiting to jump out on unsuspecting ladies and – *er-um* – display their equipment' (p. 78). However, this also shows an unsettling tendency to equate sex with aggression; a habit that is also sometimes evident in Prior's exchanges with Sarah.

 CHECK THE POEM
Many women were very active in persuading young men to join up and 'do their bit'. Jessie Pope, a popular poet whose work was published in the *Daily Mail*, wrote rousing verses such as 'The Call', which begins: 'Who's for the trench – / Are you, my laddie?'

Barker stresses Prior's intelligence throughout the **narrative**. Unlike Sassoon, he possesses insight, which is **symbolically** indicated by his association with the **image** of the eye. When he finally recalls the traumatic event that triggered his breakdown – picking up an eyeball and seeing it resting in the palm of his hand – Prior not only regains his memory, but also becomes associated with the concept of vision in general. The recurring image of the eye in the palm of his hand represents not only his recovered hindsight, but also his ability to move between a variety of different viewpoints and 'see' both sides. Because of his difference from the other characters, with regards to his class background, his opinions and his sexuality, Prior's perspective on the war is distinctive, and the source of his unique ability to subject even his own doctor to rigorous and relentless interrogation. In *Regeneration*'s sequel, *The Eye in the Door*, in which, in his role as a military intelligence gatherer, he both watches and is watched by others, Prior's association with sight is brought to the foreground of the narrative.

SARAH LUMB

CHECK THE BOOK

Women at War, edited by Nigel Fountain as part of the Imperial War Museum's 'Voices from the Twentieth Century' series (2002), includes first-hand recollections from the women who participated in the war effort during 1914–18.

If Billy Prior is distinctive because of his class, Sarah is equally so because of her gender. *Regeneration*, for the most part, depicts a world of men in which women are remarkable only by their absence. Sarah, however, represents another view of war which in many ways contradicts the official, male-authored, account. For her, the war is a liberation from the drudgery of domestic service and the restrictions of marriage. Although Barker does not gloss over the long hours of toil required of a worker in the munitions factories, through her depiction of Sarah she also emphasises the financial and social freedom that the war brought many women. Sarah earns five times more than she used to as a domestic servant, and takes full advantage of the relaxation of the sexual and social restrictions placed upon all women in peacetime. Although Sarah has been bereaved, having lost a boyfriend at the Battle of Loos, she does not let her life become constricted by mourning.

Sarah first meets Billy Prior in a café in Edinburgh, and it is significant that she makes the first move, intriguing him by her 'direct, almost boyish' attitude (p. 89). She is unimpressed by his officer status, and is not at all coy or shy in her manner, with the result that Prior is not sure 'what to make of her' (p. 90). And it is she that dictates the terms of their sexual encounters, refusing to engage in full intercourse on the night of their first meeting.

Sarah's lack of sexual inhibition can come as a surprise to the reader of *Regeneration*, who might assume that women of that period obeyed a stricter moral code. However, from the beginning of her career, Barker has been interested in writing about aspects of women's lives that contradict familiar stereotypes. She has always specialised in creating female figures who are coarse, harshly realistic, and anything but 'ladylike'. Sarah scorns her mother's view that she made a mistake in not getting engaged to her soldier boyfriend in order to ensure that she was entitled to a pension on his death, and appears to have little intention of getting married in the interests of social respectability and financial security. Nevertheless, she is a romantic, as her final declaration of love to Prior indicates – although Barker leaves the future of their relationship uncertain.

It is through Sarah that we see the real cost of the First World War as if for the first time since, like most civilians, its worst horrors are hidden from her. When she walks by mistake into a closed hospital ward full of amputees, it is an enormous shock to her. Forceful, opinionated and determined, Sarah is rarely at a loss as to what to say or do, but here the 'totally blank stare' (p. 160) of the mutilated soldiers reminds her of the impossible situation in which women are placed – deliberately excluded from the business of war, yet at the same time resented for their ignorance: 'Simply by being there, by being that inconsequential, infinitely powerful creature: *a pretty girl*, she had made everything worse' (p. 160). Sarah reacts with fury – helpless to change their view of her, and angry at her own lack of knowledge. Only Prior recognises the strength of her response, thinking that, 'She might not know much about the war, but what she did know she faced honestly' (p. 163).

WILFRED OWEN

Wilfred Owen could not be described as a fully developed character, since he appears in the novel only in a few isolated episodes, and always alongside Sassoon. Thus, he is more important

> **CONTEXT**
>
> The Great War was responsible for drastically reducing the number of marriageable young men, and the population census of 1921 revealed nearly two million single women in Britain. The next census showed that fifty per cent of these 'surplus women' were still unmarried ten years later.

CONTEXT

Interviewed for the journal *Sight and Sound* on the release of the film of *Regeneration* in 1997, Pat Barker referred to Owen as 'lower middle class in his family origins – very borderline officer material. He got in because he'd been abroad and he joined the Artist's Rifles. If he'd tried to join in England he may not have got a commission' ('Temporary Gentlemen', p. 24).

as a device for bringing out aspects of Sassoon's own character. In particular, he provides Sassoon with an artistic partner with whom he can engage in dialogue regarding the form and function of war poetry.

Even Owen's entry into the novel is unassuming, when Sassoon looks up to see a 'short, dark-haired man sid[ling] round the door' of his room (p. 80). Owen is initially cast in the role of Sassoon's subordinate or inferior – a would-be poet who regards Sassoon with admiration, even hero-worship. Sassoon does not just outclass Owen artistically, but also socially: one of the things that intimidates Owen the most is Sassoon's 'clipped, aristocratic voice' and 'bored expression' (p. 81). This is the only indication that Barker gives the reader of Owen's own background, which is middle, not upper, class, and is an example of the way in which she leaves her readers to bring their own historical knowledge of Owen to bear on their understanding of her fictional reworking. This technique is more obvious in Owen's case than in Sassoon's, since his is the more abbreviated character.

Yet this may indicate an awareness on Barker's part that, in a contemporary context, Owen is the better-known poet. In an interview she said that she found Owen a particularly difficult historical figure to translate into fiction because he 'comes with his own preexisting myth' (Sheryl Stevenson, 'With the Listener in Mind', *Critical Perspectives on Pat Barker*, 2005, p. 176). In her description of the process whereby Sassoon encourages Owen to see war as an appropriate subject for poetry, and helps him to develop one of his most famous poems, 'Anthem for Doomed Youth', Barker is portraying Sassoon's part in developing a literary reputation that will equal, or even surpass, his own. By the later part of the novel, Owen is demonstrating greater confidence in his own ideas, and is assuming a more equal artistic partnership with Sassoon. According to Daniel W. Hipp in *The Poetry of Shell Shock* (2005), Owen not only **symbolically** discovered his poetic voice under Sassoon's guidance, but also recovered his physical fluency, losing the 'slight stammer' Sassoon noted he possessed at their first meeting (see *Siegfried's Journey, 1916–1920*, 1945, p. 58).

Regeneration also makes reference to Owen's growing personal attachment to his mentor. The scene in which the two men share a final meal before Owen leaves Craiglockhart in order to return to the front is – on Owen's part at least – full of unvoiced intimacy. The fact that his deeper feelings for Sassoon remain unexpressed indicate that, while war has become a fit subject for poetic expression, love between men remains an emotion that cannot be publicly spoken or written about. Barker's representation of this event follows the two men's published recollections closely, and their emotional reticence reproduces the uncertainties surrounding the nature of their relationship. The real Owen's private letters express a heartfelt devotion for Sassoon, writing to him on 5 November 1917 that 'I love you, dispassionately, so much, so very much' (*Wilfred Owen: Collected Letters*, 1967, p. 505). Sassoon, however, was more reserved in his description of his feelings, describing Owen in his autobiography *Siegfried's Journey, 1916–1920* as someone 'of high significance to me both as poet and friend' (p. 63). Although he was to play a prominent role in ensuring the growth of Owen's posthumous literary reputation, Sassoon's critics and biographers differ on whether Owen's feelings of love were reciprocated.

DAVID BURNS

Of all the characters in *Regeneration*, it is Burns who most clearly expresses the pure horror of warfare. Based upon an actual figure treated by Rivers, Burns's experience is repellent in the extreme, and even Rivers can find 'no redeeming feature' (p. 19) that will enable him to help Burns come to terms with it. Unlike Prior, whose problem is that he has forgotten the event that led to his breakdown, Burns cannot escape the memory of being buried alive in a rotting corpse. Everything he attempts to eat brings back the 'taste and smell' of 'decomposing human flesh' (p. 19), and every night he relives the experience in his dreams. Two surreal episodes in the novel in particular emphasise this sense that Burns is stranded within his traumatic past. When he strips himself naked in the countryside outside Craiglockhart and when he confronts the 'squat and menacing' tower (p. 180) on the Suffolk coast, the contents of his mind become imprinted on the landscape, transforming it into the image of the battlefield he cannot leave behind.

> **CONTEXT**
>
> Barker is particularly interested in what she calls Owen's 'extraordinary posthumous career', saying that 'A lot of writers get stuck in their own time. They're of immense significance to their contemporaries, but they somehow don't translate. … I think that Wilfred Owen didn't get stuck in 1917 or 1918 or 1919, he got stuck in 1963, which is quite an achievement when you think he'd been dead for 40 years!' ('Detachment can be a means of survival', *Independent*, 29 March 2002).

For Rivers, Burns's tragedy is made even worse by the 'occasional glimpse of the cheerful and likeable man he must once have been' (p. 18). This sense of waste is intensified when Rivers visits him at his family home in Aldeburgh and is reminded of what Burns's life would have been like if the war had not happened: 'Twenty-two. He should be worrying about the Tripos and screwing up his courage to ask a girl to the May ball' (p. 174). The novel ends with Burns's future left uncertain. Whatever recovery he does make will be by his own efforts, since he is beyond Rivers's power to cure.

THEMES

SPEECH AND SILENCE

CONTEXT

In *Pat Barker*, Sharon Monteith writes that in the *Regeneration* trilogy 'Barker emphasizes that language cannot make immediate sense of the war; neither religious discourse nor heroic anthem says the unspeakable' (2002, p. 68).

Regeneration begins by reproducing the text of Siegfried Sassoon's Declaration, which is an early indication of its interest in the theme of protest. This is immediately followed, however, by a conversation between Rivers and Bryce, the Commandant of Craiglockhart, which makes it evident that the authorities' main concern is with the question of how to silence Sassoon's dissenting voice. It is evident that an individual does not have to be literally prevented from speaking in order to be effectively silenced – all that is necessary is to ensure that he or she will not be listened to. In Sassoon's case, this is done by sending him to a shell-shock hospital, thus implying that his antiwar protest is nothing more than the product of an unbalanced mind. It is for this reason that Rivers is given the task of determining whether Sassoon is genuinely suffering from shell-shock, or, if not, persuading him to give up his pacifist beliefs and return to the front line.

In this context, it is ironic that the method of therapy Rivers specialises in is known as the 'talking cure'. The novel features numerous instances of this technique in action, in which he encourages his patients to speak about their traumatic experiences in order to help them towards a state of acceptance. It is Rivers himself who remains silent during these conversations, a role that Billy Prior describes as acting like 'a strip of empathic wallpaper' (p. 51). Rivers prides himself on allowing his patients to unburden themselves and to speak freely, but his role in bringing Sassoon to the point where he is prepared to return to the front causes him to question whether he is actually censoring their ability to say anything of meaning.

Indeed, silence can be as eloquent as speech in *Regeneration*. Many of the characters suffer from some kind of difficulty speaking – Owen stammers; Prior is mute when he is admitted to Craiglockhart; Yealland's patient Callan is also dumb. As Rivers observes, 'Mutism seems to spring from a conflict between *wanting* to say something, and knowing that if you *do* say it the consequences will be disastrous. So you resolve it by making it physically impossible for yourself to speak' (p. 96). Stammering originates 'from the same kind of conflict as mutism, a conflict between wanting to speak and knowing that w-what you've got to say is not acceptable' (p. 97). Afraid or unwilling to speak out, the shell-shock victim's body takes on a disturbing power of expression, communicating its protest in a variety of non-verbal ways. The return of their power of speech may seemingly signify that such men are 'cured', but it also robs them of even their half-articulated rebellion against a war that requires them to risk both their lives and their sanity.

CONTEXT

In her 'Author's Note' at the end of *Regeneration*, Barker cites Elaine Showalter's *The Female Malady* and Eric Leed's *No Man's Land* as 'Two modern texts which contain stimulating discussions of "shell-shock"' (p. 251).

This is exemplified in Rivers's witnessing of Lewis Yealland's treatment of Callan, which dramatically demonstrates the **paradox** whereby a man is silenced by the very process of being given back his voice. Callan is subjected to a great deal of pain in order to compel him to overcome the unconscious prohibition against speech; yet at the same time Yealland is careful to stress that he will not be listened to when he does. The effect of this statement is to ensure that, like Sassoon, Callan's words are robbed of any subversive force, and the only speech that will be heard is that which signals his subordination to military authority.

For Rivers this is a disturbing indication of his own complicity with a system that will not allow dissent:

Just as Yealland silenced the unconscious protest of *his* patients by removing the paralysis, the deafness, the blindness, the muteness that stood between them and the war, so, in an infinitely more gentle way, *he* silenced *his* patients; for the stammerings, the nightmares, the tremors, the memory lapses, of officers were just as much unwitting protest as the grosser maladies of the men. (p. 238)

Yet Rivers, too, knows what it is to be silenced. As Billy Prior points out, if he is telling his patients that stammering indicates a fear of speaking out, then Rivers must also be experiencing the same fear. Rivers's speech-therapist father spent years listening to his son's speech in an attempt to correct his chronic stutter, yet was never interested in the meaning behind the words. And at the end of *Regeneration* there is a strong suggestion that Rivers has been silenced once again, when he can do nothing else but sign the form that records the fact that Sassoon has been passed fit for active service. It is as if Sassoon's protest had never been made, and Rivers knows that he has played a part in that process. Barker herself has said that the novel 'actually ends, in a sense, with a silencing of Rivers. He comes to write the final word for now on Sassoon, and he says there is nothing more he wanted to say that he could say. So, in the end, Rivers is silenced, too' (quoted in Donna Perry, *Backtalk: Women Writers Speak Out*, 1993, p. 55).

MASCULINITY

The persistent silencing of the male characters throughout *Regeneration* indicates the extent to which they experience feelings of disempowerment and helplessness. If masculinity is defined through the ability to dominate and control, then none of the men in the novel are truly masculine. Barker draws our attention to the way in which the war itself has become responsible for this situation, in which thousands of men are broken, traumatised and in crisis.

The First World War has introduced new rules for warfare that prohibit decisive action. Billy Prior is extremely scornful of officers who 'somewhere at the back of their ... *tiny tiny* minds ... really do believe the whole thing's going to end in one big glorious *cavalry charge*' (p. 66); yet that is precisely how boys were brought up to define military heroism before 1914. Instead, modern technological

CHECK THE POEM

In 'The Repression of War Experience', published in *Counter-Attack and Other Poems*, Sassoon creates an evocative portrayal of war trauma.

war involves 'crouching in a dugout waiting to be killed. The war that had promised so much in the way of "manly" activity had actually delivered "feminine" passivity, and on a scale that their mothers and sisters had scarcely known. No wonder they broke down' (pp. 107–8). The condition of shell-shock is directly related to the constant strain and tensions of trench fighting, but neither the military machine nor the soldiers themselves see it that way. Instead, they regard shell-shock as a shaming condition that makes those who suffer from it something less than 'proper' men.

A good example of this in *Regeneration* is Anderson's description of his dream of wearing ladies' corsets, which **symbolically** expresses Anderson's deep anxiety regarding his masculine identity. The principal symptom of his war trauma, a deeply rooted phobia of blood, not only makes it impossible for him to continue to work as an army doctor, but also affects his long-term ability to provide for his wife and child. Another of Rivers's patients, Willard, steadfastly refuses to admit that his paralysis is emotional in origin, since that 'would be tantamount to an admission of cowardice' (p. 112). Strong, brutal and muscular, Willard otherwise conforms to the masculine ideal, and he fumes at his physical helplessness when his wife cannot push his wheelchair up the hill, leaving him 'stranded' and 'impotent' (p. 119). Like Anderson, his inability to act as a strong figure for his wife to look up to becomes an indication of a deeper sense of disempowerment.

As well as traumatised heterosexuals, *Regeneration* abounds in characters who are homosexual or bisexual. As his conversations with Rivers demonstrate, Sassoon is self-accepting about his homosexuality – indeed, in his willingness to associate with publicly homosexual figures he is almost too open, in a period in which masculine same-sex desire was a crime – and it is an orientation shared by Wilfred Owen. Rivers's sexuality is unclear, although the strength of his attachment to Sassoon suggests that he, too, might be homosexual by inclination. Robert Graves disowns his homosexual past towards the end of the novel, when he tells Sassoon that, since meeting a girl of whom he has become fond, 'my affections have been running in more normal channels' (p. 199). Yet Graves's repudiation of homosexuality is perhaps understandable in a novel

CHECK THE POEM

In 'It's a Queer Time', Robert Graves depicts the trauma of trench life, in which one minute 'you'll be dozing safe in your dug-out', and the next 'the trench shakes and falls about'.

CHECK THE BOOK
For more information regarding sexual panic during the First World War, see pp. 9–22 of *Twentieth-Century Sexuality: A History* by Angus McLaren (1999).

which portrays a society becoming increasingly intolerant of the practice. Memories of the imprisonment of Oscar Wilde, former lover of Sassoon's friend and pacifist mentor Robert Ross, stand as an example of how severely homosexuality could be dealt with. *Regeneration* also mentions the antihomosexual crusade of the MP Pemberton Billing, which explicitly linked homosexuality to the degeneracy of British masculinity. Homosexuals are neither proper men nor proper patriots, according to Pemberton Billing, and their sexual behaviour 'make[s] their loyalty to their country suspect' (p. 204). Thus, homosexuality is not a personal and private choice, but a risky decision that sets the individual outside dominant conceptions of manliness and makes him vulnerable to prosecution and imprisonment.

THE CHANGING ROLE OF WOMEN

Regeneration portrays a world of traumatised men in a state of crisis, one way or the other, about their sexuality, and this is only rendered more acute by the contrasting experience of women in the same period. If men are losing their sense of assertion and control, women are gaining it, taking on the jobs left vacant by the men who have gone to fight, and gaining a new self-confidence.

Sarah Lumb and her friends become Barker's personifications of this freedom. Billy Prior comes across them in an Edinburgh café, his amnesiac, asthmatic and solitary state in clear contrast to their cheerful vitality. Their work at the munitions factory gives them economic independence, and a world without men has left them space to flourish socially.

However, it is important to realise that these women are still living within certain constraints, even if they are rather looser than they were before the war began. When Sarah's mother voices concerns that her daughter's behaviour will affect her chances of getting a husband, she draws attention to the temporary nature of Sarah's wartime role. Once the conflict has ended, the men will return to resume their civilian occupations, and women will find themselves with no choice but to return to their former lives. Moreover, in spite of their new-found freedom, women are still subject to their own reproductive functions, as the story of Betty, who botches a self-administered abortion attempt, graphically demonstrates. The war, it is obvious, has made it no more acceptable for a woman to have a child outside marriage than it was before.

Although the actual female characters in this novel are down-to-earth, pragmatic figures, Barker also demonstrates how, when regarded through the eyes of men, women tend to become 'Woman': a symbolic figure on which to pin stereotyped male-authored fantasies of womanhood. In her depiction of Sarah, in particular, Barker shows how the mundane details of Sarah's everyday life are unimportant to Prior, who demonstrates a recurring tendency to make her represent aspects of his own fears or prejudices. Like the huge majority of other women of the period, Sarah does not, it is true, have first-hand experience of front-line fighting, but that is hardly something for which she can be blamed. And she may know more than she is given credit for – when she stumbles across the horribly wounded men hidden away in a remote hospital ward, she does not run away out of horror, but anger at 'being forced to play the role of Medusa when she meant no harm' (p. 160). What *Regeneration* suggests is that there is a world of female experience that simply does not appear in public accounts of the First World War, which are predominantly produced by men.

FATHERS

Fathers are largely absent from the world of *Regeneration*, but that does not stop them having an enormous – and often catastrophic – effect upon the lives of their sons. Prior's father makes a brief appearance in Rivers's office, but he seems to Rivers 'to have no feeling for his son at all, except contempt' (p. 57). Sassoon's father left his family when Sassoon was a small child, and his early death leaves Sassoon feeling abandoned. Rivers's own deceased father appears in his son's recollections as a strict disciplinarian who upheld standards Rivers found impossible to live up to.

The biological fathers in this novel are representatives of a higher power, from whom they gain their authority and symbolic force. When Rivers goes to church while staying at his brother's house, his

CONTEXT

The traditional role of women is summed up in the well-known popular song 'Keep the Home Fires Burning', which was composed by Ivor Novello in 1915. It entreated a female audience to: 'Keep the home fires burning, / While your hearts are yearning, / Though your lads are far away / They dream of home'.

 CHECK THE POEM

One of Siegfried Sassoon's most famous poems, 'The Glory of Women', attacks women for their unthinking support of the war and their ignorance of its horrors.

According to
Christian beliefs,
God allowed his
son Jesus to be
born as a human
being in order
that he might be
sacrificed to save
humanity from its
sinful state. It is
summed up in the
Bible in the Book
of John, Chapter
3, verse 6: 'For
God had such love
for the world that
he gave his only
Son, so that
whoever has faith
in him may not
come to
destruction but
have eternal life'.

contemplation of the stained glass window above the altar shows
the extent to which submission to the authority of the father is
woven into Western belief systems. The window's depiction of the
biblical story of Abraham and Isaac, alongside the image of the
crucifixion, represents for Rivers 'the two bloody bargains on which
a civilization claims to be based' (p. 149) – that is, the son's
agreement to obey the father in return for the promise that he will
eventually inherit the father's authority. The war is the ultimate test
of the strength of this bargain, and the fact that it holds, even under
such extreme circumstances, is frightening. Sons are going to war in
obedience to their fathers' request, but are not surviving to take
their place. Instead, 'the inheritors were dying, not one by one,
while old men, and women of all ages, gathered together and sang
hymns' (p. 149). In this context, the concept of 'country' itself is
gendered male, with soldiers sacrificing themselves for the
'fatherland'.

The concept of the actual flesh-and-blood father is thus replaced
with the abstract figure of the **patriarch**, the ultimate **symbol** of
masculine authority. All the male characters in the novel exist in
submission to this concept, and their compulsion to obey
contributes towards their sense of emasculation. Viewed in this
context, shell-shock may represent an attempt to rebel, for if the
patriarch controls speech – what is said, by whom, and who is
listened to – then the inarticulacy of the traumatised soldiers could
be the only way left open to them through which to express their
fear and anger. Even this, though, is stifled by the intervention of
the therapist, whose job is to silence such protests and return men
to a 'proper' sense of duty.

There is, then, no single character in this book who can be said to
fully represent patriarchal authority. Instead, the male figures tend
to be both the disobedient son *and* the father who compels
obedience. Rivers may have resented his father's attempts to control
his speech, and by implication his thoughts, yet he realises that he
demands the same thing of his patients. Sassoon is an abandoned
son, but also an inspirational officer who leads his men into battle in
obedience to the commands of those above him. Instead, the notion
of 'authority' tends to be presented as essentially disembodied, with

the result that it is nowhere yet everywhere – and this has the effect
of making it far more difficult to resist.

Indeed, the most explicit manifestation of patriarchal authority in
the novel is a symbolic one. When Burns goes missing from his
house in Suffolk in the middle of a stormy night, Rivers finds him
staring up at a tower situated in the middle of marshland by the
coast. The tower is sinister and unsettling, 'squat and unimpressive',
yet 'menacing' (p. 179), and as Burns's traumatised gaze is focused
upon it, it 'gleam[s] white, like the bones of a skull' (p. 180). It thus
becomes, quite literally 'the place of the skull', or Golgotha, the site
at which Christ allowed himself to be sacrificed at his father's
command; just as the boy-soldiers of the First World War obeyed
the directives that sent them to the battlefields. But whereas in the
Christian story Christ rises again as the saviour of mankind, here
there is no redemption and no renewal: only death.

Even the isolated instances of positive fathering in *Regeneration* are
overshadowed by this idea. This is seen particularly in the
relationship between Rivers and Sassoon, in which Sassoon comes
to regard Rivers as 'his father confessor' (p. 145). He realises 'how
completely Rivers ha[s] come to take his father's place', and decides
that 'if it came to substitute fathers, he might do a lot worse'
(p. 145). Rivers's compassion towards all his patients causes him to
be regarded as a beneficial fatherly presence, and he worries over
the welfare of men like Burns, and even Prior, as if they were his
children. But however compassionate his motives might be, the fact
remains that all his efforts are directed towards returning them to an
awareness of their duty. As the novel progresses, Rivers agonises
more and more about whether he is in fact betraying the men for
whom he cares so deeply.

 QUESTION

Do you think
Regeneration
shows that Rivers's
motives are
superior to
Yealland's, or are
they ultimately the
same?

REGENERATION

The motif of regeneration is introduced into the novel through
Rivers's recollections of his prewar experiments with Henry Head
into the regeneration of nerves. A nerve in Head's own arm is
severed, and Rivers has to chart the healing process, a task which
often involves causing Head extreme pain. Rivers does not enjoy
this, but he does it anyway, in the belief that the knowledge is worth

acquiring. The essential lesson gained from this experiment is, first, that the process of healing invariably causes suffering to the patient; and, second, that the therapist should not shy away from inflicting pain if it helps the patient progress towards an ultimate recovery. The memory of this event helps Rivers to cope with the distress he feels when witnessing the suffering of shell-shocked soldiers, which he often feels he is only intensifying in the course of his efforts to cure them: 'In advising them to remember the traumatic events that had led to their being sent here, he was, in effect, inflicting pain, and doing so in pursuit of a treatment that he knew to be still largely experimental' (p. 47).

But the question of who, or what, is being regenerated in the course of the novel remains largely unanswered by its end. Whether any of the protagonists can be described as having been truly 'healed' remains in doubt. Sassoon has decided to return to France, but has not given up his protest, and Rivers fears that these 'internal divisions' (p. 249) might lead to either a 'real breakdown' (p. 250), or cause him to submit to a 'genuine and very deep desire for death' (p. 250). Burns remains a shell of the bright young man he once was, and Prior's role as misfit is only intensified by his removal from active service. Even Rivers, whose views on the war and his own role within it undergo a process of change as the novel progresses, does not end it with any firm sense of resolution. Thus, rather than extending the promise of a cure, regeneration is descriptive of an unfinished process whose ultimate end cannot be fully envisaged.

Moreover, there are suggestions contained within the novel that regeneration is not always a positive concept. After all, the name of the hospital magazine, the *Hydra*, is a reference to the multi-headed monster of Greek mythology who could not be killed due to its ability to regrow its severed heads. Viewed in this context, perhaps regeneration does not lead to positive renewal so much as never-ending conflict; a conclusion reinforced by readers' knowledge that the First World War was only the first conflict of the twentieth century, and was far from 'the war to end all wars'.

CHECK THE NET
The hydra is reproduced on the November 1917 cover of the first edition of the *Hydra* magazine, where it is depicted as battling with a shell-shocked patient. For a reproduction of the image, and an invitation to further analysis, see the website of Napier University's War Poets Collection at **www2.napier.ac. uk/warpoets**. Click on 'Education', 'Intermediate-2 and Higher Level', and then 'The Monster Within?'

SETTING

Although the action of *Regeneration* moves between a variety of
settings, such as London, Edinburgh and Suffolk, the majority of
it is rooted in a single location – Craiglockhart Military Hospital.
Like the novel's characters, the hospital itself is an imaginary
recreation of reality. It really did exist, and its buildings, now part
of Napier University, remain in use and can be visited. Originally
built in 1877, Craiglockhart was a hydropathic hospital; that is, a
centre for water-based alternative therapy treatments. The
existence of an indoor swimming pool, made use of by Sassoon
and Graves in Chapter 4, is evidence of the building's past. The
title of the hospital magazine edited for a while by Wilfred
Owen, the *Hydra*, while the name of the nine-headed monster
of Greek mythology – as discussed in **Themes: Regeneration**
above – is also a pun on Craiglockhart's 'hydro'pathic origins.
The hospital was requisitioned by the military in 1916, and
remained an institution for the treatment of shell-shocked officers
until 1919.

In spite of the fact that it is a real place with a real history,
Craiglockhart as Barker portrays it in *Regeneration* is also a highly
symbolic site where fact and fantasy exist side by side, and this
makes it a very inconsistent, and at times ghostly, place. In one
sense, the walls of the building confine its inhabitants, for although
it is not a prison, it maintains a military discipline. The comings and
goings of the patients are monitored (as Prior discovers when he is
punished for returning late after a night out in Edinburgh), and they
are expected to wear full uniform at all times. In Chapter 9, for
example, the Head of Office Administration sees some of the men
cutting the lawn without their shirts, tunics and ties on and
commands them to redress, despite the heat and the apparent
informality of the occasion.

But however strong its walls appear to be, Craiglockhart is also
'decayed' (p. 142), which suggests that it conceals a disturbing
fragility behind its apparent solidity. While the institution's rules
and regulations are strictly enforced, the minds of its inhabitants

CONTEXT

Barker's depiction
of Craiglockhart is
indebted to
Sassoon's portrayal
of the hospital he
calls 'Slateford' in
Sherston's Progress
(1936). Gloomy
enough by day,
when it possesses
'the melancholy
atmosphere of a
decayed hydro', at
night it becomes
'sepulchral and
oppressive with
saturations of
war experience'
(p. 556).

cannot be as easily controlled. Consequently, Barker depicts it as a place haunted by visions of the dead and memories of war, the backdrop of the fears, dreams and delusions of the traumatised men it contains. It is a place of 'screams and running footsteps' (p. 63) in which, while there is little physical privacy, each person is isolated in his or her own neurotic world.

As discussed in **Language and style** below, Barker tells her story mainly through dialogue. This means that Craiglockhart is never described in any detail, only envisaged through the reactions of those who visit, work and are treated there. For instance, when Robert Graves arrives at the hospital, he looks at its 'massive yellow-gray façade' and is shocked (p. 20). Barker does not tell the reader anything more about what the building looks like, leaving it up to us to infer what he means by his reaction. This adds to Barker's **paradoxical** portrayal of her setting, which is at once a military institution and a haunted house; real, yet also imaginary; a place of dread, but also of healing.

LANGUAGE AND STYLE

Barker is renowned for the apparent simplicity of her writing style, which rejects complex vocabulary and syntax in favour of plain, even terse, sentence construction. This is directly linked to her preference for telling her story through dialogue, a technique that serves her extremely well in *Regeneration*. Rivers's exchanges with his patients are central to the novel, entire chapters of which consist of little more than conversation. The text is anchored in the language of everyday speech, excluding the use of a more 'mannered' or stylised **narrative** voice.

This is reinforced by Barker's habitual omission of the **reporting clause** in the conversations she depicts, thus moving her own role as author even further into the background. Take, for example, this exchange between Rivers and Prior in Chapter 7:

CONTEXT

In an interview for the women's writing magazine *Mslexia*, Barker said that she deliberately does not write in difficult prose because, 'as a first generation university graduate', she 'wants to go on talking on equal terms and with total respect to people who had to leave school at fifteen' (Issue 5, Spring/Summer 2000).

'All right. I'll see you tomorrow.'

'It isn't fair to say I don't want treatment. I've asked for treatment and you've refused to give it me.'

Rivers looked blank. 'Oh, I see. The hypnosis. I didn't think you were serious.'

'Why shouldn't I be serious? It is used to recover lost memory, isn't it?'

'Ye-es.'

'So why won't you do it?' (p. 68)

Nowhere in this conversation does Barker tell us who is speaking, or in what tone – instead, we have to infer this information for ourselves. However, it is extremely effective at economically conveying the quick to-and-fro rhythm of the dialogue between the two men, from which we can deduce a great deal of information regarding their characters and relationship. Prior's relentless questioning of Rivers makes him appear blunt and belligerent, while Rivers's slower speech patterns (such as his hesitant 'Ye-es') indicate a desire to calm Prior down and put a stop to his rather aggressive interrogation. Rivers's dialogues with Sassoon, in contrast, are less rapid, and more conversational – and it is Rivers who asks most of the questions. In this way, Barker implies that their association is much more relaxed, with Sassoon submitting far more willingly than Prior to Rivers's medical authority.

Because Barker chooses not to use an **omniscient narrator** in *Regeneration*, we are not given a detached viewpoint on either the characters or the action. Instead, the **narrative point of view** keeps changing as we see events through the eyes of different characters, and witness what they are thinking and feeling without the apparent use of an intermediary authorial voice. When Rivers meets Willard and his wife who are unable to navigate their way back up the drive at Craiglockhart, for example, we only learn of Willard's emotional state through Rivers's perception of it: 'He felt Willard's fury at being stranded like this, impotent. Good. The more furious he was the better' (p. 119). Typically, this tells the reader as much about Rivers as it does about Willard: Rivers's alertness to Willard's emotional state is a direct consequence of his personal involvement with all his patients.

 CHECK THE NET

Wera Reusch's useful interview with Pat Barker concerning *Regeneration*, 'A Backdoor into the Present', can be found at: **www.lolapress. org**. Click 'move on', then 'electronic lola', then 'Lol@ 1' (2000) and scroll down the list.

Another hallmark of Barker's linguistic style is her ability to reproduce the patterns of working-class speech, particularly Tyneside dialect. Tyneside, in the northeast of England, is the area from which Barker herself originates, and where she has set many of her novels. Although *Regeneration*, being set in Scotland, is an exception to this, her introduction of the Geordie munitions workers Sarah Lumb and her friends enables her to bring their distinctive voices into the narrative: 'She says, "I went down the town and there was a man winked at us and I winked back. He says, 'Howay over the Moor.'" So she says, "I gans over the Moor with him," she says, "and I let him have what he wanted"' (p. 88). Barker is well aware that the literature of the First World War is dominated by the voices of men. Furthermore, the great majority of them are middle or upper class, and accordingly use the kind of standard English in their writing that is perceived as 'accentless'. Barker's use of regional dialect contradicts that, introducing the voices of working-class northern women into the narrative in order to tell another story of the war that has been excluded from mainstream accounts.

The narrative of *Regeneration* is thus very mobile, moving between the perspectives and voices of officers and munitionettes, the educated upper and the working lower classes, men and women. Because the lives of her characters vary so widely, the text contains little sense of consensus. The views of a working-class female munitions worker from Tyneside cannot be expected to coincide with those of an upper-middle-class military officer and poet from Kent, nor does Barker have any interest in hiding that fact. Instead, the widely divergent opinions and lifestyles of Sarah Lumb and Siegfried Sassoon bear testimony to Barker's central point that the war was experienced in many different ways, and all are of value.

Regeneration also self-consciously reflects upon literary style in the course of the novel itself; in particular, the appropriate way in which to represent the war in writing. This comes to the foreground in the conversations between Sassoon and Owen, in which Sassoon helps Owen to recognise that his experiences in the trenches can become the subject-matter for poetry. The rest of their association revolves around Owen's efforts to evolve a poetic voice distinct from

 QUESTION

Barker may use plain language, but she also makes frequent use of italics for emphasis in speech. Why do you think she does this?

Sassoon's, and Barker depicts the meticulous selection of words and pruning of phrases as he strives to develop a poetic discourse, which is quite different from anything he has used before. Both the mood and the language of 'Song of Songs', his first poem published in the *Hydra*, are entirely different from the poem on which Owen and Sassoon work together, 'Anthem for Doomed Youth'. Whereas the first is elegiac and highly stylised, the second expresses angry emotions and a desire to protest through the use of a more everyday discourse. Owen is no longer writing about abstract subjects, but an event on which he has developed strong, and deeply personal, opinions derived from first-hand experience. This is not a poem in which to take refuge, but one which is forcing its reader to confront uncomfortable facts about the slaughter on the Western Front.

It is significant in this context that Barker depicts the two men working on the first two lines of 'Anthem for Doomed Youth', showing the way in which, under Sassoon's urging, they become increasingly forceful. Sassoon is tempted to dismiss the first draft as sounding like 'War Office propaganda' (p. 141), and helps Owen to use more emphatic and emotive language. The most significant development occurs when Owen changes the phrase 'anger of our guns' in the poem's second line to 'anger of the guns', which then helps him to decide on 'monstrous' as the appropriate adjective. This in turn triggers an alteration to the first line: 'those who die so fast' to 'those who die in herds'. The reader who already knows the poem will recognise that it will eventually be changed again, to the even more shocking image of 'those who die as cattle'; but the finished verse is not something Barker is interested in reproducing. Instead, she is showing how the effort entailed in the production of any piece of literature is intensified when one is breaking away from tradition and attempting to write in an entirely different way. This new kind of warfare cannot be depicted through the use of poetic platitudes, but demands a revolution in both style and language.

 CHECK THE NET

'Song of Songs' demonstrates the extent to which Owen's poetic style and subject matter changed during his stay at Craiglockhart. The poem can be found on the web at **http:// users.fulladsl.be/ spb1667**. Follow the 'Owen' links.

PART FOUR

CRITICAL PERSPECTIVES

READING CRITICALLY

This section provides a range of critical viewpoints and perspectives on *Regeneration* and gives a broad overview of key debates, interpretations and theories proposed since the novel was published. It is important to bear in mind the variety of interpretations and responses this text has produced, many of them shaped by the critics' own backgrounds and historical contexts.

No single view of the text should be seen as dominant – it is important that you arrive at your own judgements by questioning the perspectives described, and by developing your own critical insights. Objective analysis is a skill achieved through coupling close reading with an informed understanding of the key ideas, related texts and background information relevant to the text. These elements are all crucial in enabling you to assess the interpretations of other readers, and even to view works of criticism as texts in themselves. The ability to read critically will serve you well both in your study of *Regeneration*, and in any critical writing, presentation or further work you undertake.

**CHECK
THE BOOK**

*Pat Barker's
Regeneration: A
Reader's Guide* by
Karin Westman
(2001) is an
accessible
introduction to the
novel, and includes
a detailed
examination of its
critical reception.

CRITICAL RECEPTION

On its publication in 1991, *Regeneration* was widely, and favourably, reviewed. Mark Wormald, writing in *The Times Literary Supplement*, went so far as to call it 'one of the most impressive novels to have appeared in recent years' (24 May 1991). Wormald also complimented Barker's deft handling of her historical sources, and her unflinching examination of the horror of war. Justine Picardie, reviewing *Regeneration* for the *Independent*, called it 'an austere and very fine novel' ('The poet who came out of his shell shock', 25 June 1991).

Regeneration received its US publication in 1992, and in *The New York Times Book Review*, Samuel Hynes regarded it as a contribution to a tradition of antiwar writing which tells 'a part of the whole story of war that is not often told – how war may batter and break men's minds' ('Among Damaged Men', 29 March 1992). He particularly praised Barker's use of literary realism, claiming that it demonstrated her to be 'a writer who is content to confront a cruel reality without polemics, without even visible anger and without evident artifice'. *The New York Times* went on to pick *Regeneration* as one of the four best novels of 1992.

Regeneration attracted little negative criticism, and what there was appeared as asides within otherwise highly complimentary reviews. Paul Taylor thought that the conversations between Owen and Sassoon were rather artificial – 'a bit like a programme for the Open University' ('Hero at the Emotional Front', *Independent on Sunday*, 2 June 1991) – while Samuel Hynes thought it ended too soon, asking 'Why not follow Sassoon to the front, where he fought again until he was wounded by one of his own men and was evacuated to England? Why not take up the story of Owen, ordered back to France to fight in the final assault, and killed in action a week before the Armistice?' This was, of course, answered by Barker in *The Eye in the Door* and *The Ghost Road*, the books that continue the story of her characters in *Regeneration*, and that had the effect of prolonging critical considerations of the earlier novel.

Interestingly, most reviewers treated Sassoon as *Regeneration*'s central figure. Only Paul Taylor's review focused specifically on Rivers as the character around whom all the other figures in the novel revolve. According to Taylor, 'the central characterization of Rivers is excellent', and Barker's portrayal reveals him to be 'one of the heroes of the Great War'.

Regeneration was not regarded as a controversial text, although Karin Westman writes that Siegfried Sassoon's son George apparently criticised Barker for 'basing her depiction of his famous father too closely on Sassoon's autobiographical novel *The Complete Memoirs of George Sherston*' (*Pat Barker's Regeneration*, 2001, p. 83). However, Barker's publisher appears to have proved

> **CONTEXT**
>
> The bells were ringing to celebrate the end of the war when Owen's mother received the telegram informing her of her son's death.

> **CONTEXT**
>
> In spite of embarking on a series of homosexual affairs after the First World War, Sassoon married Hester Gatty in 1933. George was their only child, and the couple separated in 1945.

that no copyright laws had been violated in Barker's portrayal of Sassoon, as the issue went no further.

Reviewers were almost unanimous in seeing the novel as a notable change of direction for Barker. For example, Justine Picardie begins by explaining that 'Pat Barker is best known as a feminist writer, and for her gritty tales of working-class women's lives in the north of England. Her new novel, *Regeneration*, therefore comes as a surprise: it enters a very masculine world'; a description that is closely echoed by Paul Taylor: 'Barker has specialized in gritty feminist sagas, so this book represents an admirable extension of her range'.

LATER CRITICISM

 CHECK THE NET
Pat Barker's web page on the British Council 'Contemporary Writers' website at **www. contemporary writers.com** provides an informative overview of her career. Type 'Pat Barker' into the search authors box.

The *Regeneration* trilogy as a whole, and the novel *Regeneration* in particular, played a pivotal role in establishing Pat Barker as an important twentieth-century author. Very little literary criticism was published on her writing prior to 1991, and academic interest was clearly aroused by the commercial success of *Regeneration* and its sequels. As has already been discussed, the first reviews of *Regeneration* were unanimous in their claim that the novel represented a shift in Barker's work away from an exclusive concern with female characters and women's experience, to the representation of masculine worlds and an interest in war, conflict and psychological trauma. These became – and continue to be – the main themes explored by literary critics interested in Barker's work. Furthermore, any survey of the criticism published on Barker will show that the *Regeneration* trilogy remains, even now, the most frequently discussed of Barker's texts.

Nevertheless, most detailed criticism of the novel did not begin to surface until around five years after its original publication, which, given the enthusiasm of the original reviews, seems somewhat puzzling. There are, however, three significant reasons for this critical timelag. First, and most obviously, the success of *The Ghost Road*, which was published in 1995, and won the Booker Prize for that year, further cemented Barker's reputation as a major British author, and the completion of this third book allowed the three First World War texts to be considered as a trilogy.

Second, the film adaptation of *Regeneration*, directed by Gillies MacKinnon, and starring Jonathan Pryce as Rivers and Jonny Lee Miller as Prior, was released in 1997, drawing further critical attention to Barker's work. Although it was not a huge commercial success, it received a BAFTA nomination for Best British Film. Barker did not write the screenplay herself, but she was very involved with the film's production, and was clearly pleased with the result. In an interview entitled 'Temporary Gentlemen' published in *Sight and Sound* in 1997, Mark Sinker noted that Barker 'appears comfortable with both [the film making] process and the result' (p. 22), even though some elements of her original plot were omitted.

CHECK THE FILM
The film version of *Regeneration* was released in the US in a substantially edited version entitled *Behind the Lines*.

Third, and perhaps most significantly, the *Regeneration* trilogy was completed at a time when public anxiety was being voiced over whether the Great War would continue to be remembered. By the late 1990s it was rapidly passing out of living memory, yet the act of remembering the cost of war seemed more necessary than ever, given the conflict in the Gulf and the growing tension between Albanians and Serbs in Kosovo, which was to erupt into war in 1998. In an attempt to draw the younger generation into Remembrance Day commemorations, the Spice Girls became the faces of the Poppy Appeal for 1997. From 1919 onwards, it was customary to observe a two-minute silence on the Sunday closest to the date on which the Armistice was signed – 11 November – a day known as Remembrance Sunday. But during the 1990s, the British Legion successfully campaigned for the two-minute silence to also be held on 11 November itself, indicating an expansion of the observation of remembrance in British culture.

One of the earliest full-length critical essays appeared in the prestigious *New Yorker* magazine in 1996, written by Blake Morrison. The final novel in the *Regeneration* trilogy, *The Ghost Road*, had just been published in the US, and Morrison took this event as an opportunity to conduct a survey of Barker's life and her literary career. He reinforced the opinion already voiced in reviews that the *Regeneration* trilogy was something of a departure from her previous works, which tended to centre upon the lives of working-class women, not 'dead white European males' ('War Stories', p. 78). Morrison's analysis of *Regeneration* focuses upon her portrayals of Rivers and of Billy Prior, whom Morrison regards as one of Barker's 'greatest assets' (p. 80). One of the elements in the trilogy that clearly intrigues Morrison is the contrast between the author and her subject-matter, and he marvels at the fact that 'a middle-aged woman' can write about sex 'with candor and sensuality' (p. 80). For Morrison, this is linked to her writing style, which uses everyday rather than stylised literary language. He points out that she does not recreate the actual way in which officers of the First World War, in particular, would have spoken: instead, they use 'current idiom' (p. 80). This, argues Morrison, actually makes Barker's portrayals of her characters more convincing, because 'what she loses in historical accuracy she gains in linguistic vitality, eroding the discontinuities between then and now' (p. 80). In this way, the trilogy isn't just recreating a historical period, but is creating links between past and present.

? QUESTION

In what ways do the past and the present collide in *Regeneration*?

Subsequent critics came to focus, however, on two aspects of *Regeneration* that Morrison does not: its representations of gender and of trauma. In 1998, Greg Harris published an essay entitled 'Compulsory Masculinity, Britain and the Great War: The Literary-Historical Work of Pat Barker' in the academic journal *Critique*. It focuses on the link between shell-shock and masculinity, whereby the act of breaking down breaks unwritten codes dictating appropriate male behaviour, which require the soldier to suppress expressions of shock and emotion no matter what horrors he witnesses. Harris argues that Rivers and Sassoon, in the novel as in life, are both well trained in emotional repression, but that Barker uses her historical source material to 'expose the ways in which masculinity was manipulated during wartime' (p. 292). She does this by portraying the way in which Rivers, in particular, begins to accept the necessity of expressing emotion as a way of coping with the stress of warfare: 'Rivers's encouragement of feelings such as tenderness and love for fellow soldiers, seems invariably to have led these men on journeys of introspective exploration into unpaved avenues of emotion never before taken or even thought available' (p. 295).

Prior is also important in the process of revealing how masculine codes were maintained and challenged during the war, his extreme difficulty in expressing an emotional response indicative of 'the emotional crippling that Prior and Rivers, as males, have been culturally inscribed to endure' (p. 298). Thus, for Harris, Barker demonstrates that to be a man within a patriarchal order does not 'necessarily equate to a general empowerment'. Instead, 'patriarchal constructions of masculinity colonize men's subjectivity in ways that, especially in wartime, prove oppressive, repressive, and wholly brutal in their effects on the male psyche' (p. 303).

Also in 1998, Anne Whitehead published an essay in *Modern Fiction Studies* which exemplified the second main topic focused on by critics of *Regeneration*: its portrayal of trauma and its treatment. In 'Open to Suggestion: Hypnosis and History in Pat Barker's *Regeneration*', Whitehead, who is a specialist in psychoanalytic and trauma theory at Newcastle University, focuses on Barker's representation of hypnosis in the novel. She outlines the debates surrounding the use of hypnosis to treat shell-shock victims in the First World War, and argues that it becomes, like Rivers's dream analysis, a means of bringing the past into the present. Having hypnotised Prior, 'Rivers acts to reconstruct the forgotten event in Prior's past, which Prior is then able to reclaim and integrate into his identity' (p. 688). However, Barker does not allow this process to provide an unproblematic answer to Prior's problems, and Whitehead argues that Prior's rage at what he sees as the triviality of the event that has caused his breakdown 'raises the question of the historical status of the traumatic event: Prior's narrative appears to him to be more immediate, more real than the memory of the past that he uncovers' (p. 689). In other words, what actually happened to Prior is not as 'real' as what he *imagines* had happened, and this in turn causes the reader to question the reliability of historical accounts. The result is a depiction of the past as 'based on notions of narrative and authorship', enabling it to 'become the site for a number of competing fictions' (p. 689).

Book-length studies of Barker's work have not appeared until relatively recently. In 2001, Karin Westman published a brief 'Reader's Guide' to *Regeneration*, but the first full-length book on

 CHECK THE NET
For further discussion of Barker's portrayal of masculinity in *Regeneration*, see Peter Hitchcock's essay 'What is Prior?: Working-Class Masculinity in Pat Barker's Trilogy' in issue 35 of the online journal *Genders* at **www.genders.org**. Click on 'recent issues' and scroll down to the list for issue 35, then follow the link.

 CHECK THE FILM
Flashbacks also feature in *A Very Long Engagement* (2004), which stars Audrey Tautou as a young woman who searches for the truth about what happened to her fiancé during the First World War.

Barker came out the following year. Written by Sharon Monteith, *Pat Barker* was published as part of the British Council's 'Writers and their Work' series. A very useful and accessible overview of Barker's writing and career, it includes a chapter devoted to the *Regeneration* trilogy in which all its central themes are outlined. Another book, also entitled *Pat Barker*, was published by John Brannigan in 2005. Like Monteith's, it is a survey work which includes a consideration of all of Barker's novels up until *Double Vision*, published in 2003 (a text which was, naturally, excluded from Monteith's 2002 publication). The *Regeneration* trilogy is discussed in a chapter that focuses on it as 'an experimental work of historical fiction' (p. 96). What makes it 'experimental', according to Brannigan, is its destabilisation of coherent conceptions of the past through its 'heightened attention … to problems of memory, to the disturbing meanings which lie buried in the past awaiting present discovery' (p. 119). Brannigan is keen to situate Barker within a tradition of twentieth-century writing that questions the transmission and interpretation of narratives of the past, placing her alongside contemporaries such as Michèle Roberts, Ian Sinclair and Peter Ackroyd.

In terms of Barker criticism, 2005 was a particularly productive year, since as well as Brannigan's book, it saw the publication of a volume of essays entitled *Critical Perspectives on Pat Barker* edited by Sharon Monteith, Margaretta Jolly, Nahem Yousaf and Ronald Paul. Some of the pieces, such as Anne Whitehead's essay, had already been published elsewhere, while others were commissioned specifically for the volume, which indicates its ambition to bring together an internationally authored collection of both old and new essays in order to open out the critical discussion of Barker's writing. The centrality of the *Regeneration* trilogy to her career is indicated by its predominance within the collection – two out of five sections are dedicated to discussion of either the trilogy as a whole or one of its constituent volumes, and it also includes an essay on the film adaptation of *Regeneration*.

CONTEXT

Michèle Roberts (b. 1949) is a novelist, poet and short story writer, whose **narratives** frequently explore historical themes from a feminist perspective. For example, in *The Wild Girl* (1984), she imagines the story of the biblical figure of Mary Magdalene. Ian Sinclair (b. 1943) and Peter Ackroyd (b. 1949) are both well known for their recreations of London's past – specifically, its literary and cultural past – in novels such as *Hawksmoor* (Ackroyd, 1985) and *White Chappell, Scarlet Tracings* (Sinclair, 1987).

CONTEMPORARY APPROACHES

GENDER THEORY

Gender theory has arisen out of feminist investigations into the categories of sex and gender. A conservative view of sex and gender upholds the view that: 1) there are two sexes: male and female; 2) sex is biological, and thus 'natural'; and 3) gender is the outward manifestation of one's sex in a social and cultural context.

From the seventies onwards, though, feminists began to investigate gender's role as the cultural expression of sex, noting that it changes according to historical and cultural context, and therefore might be more fluid than had previously been supposed. Gayle Rubin, in her essay 'The Traffic in Women' (1975), argues that, in a **patriarchal** society, gender was naturalised by being assumed to be an inevitable consequence of biological sex. So, for example, passivity in women or aggression in men were not thought to be learnt behaviours, but to be biological in origin, and thus an automatic part of what it meant to be 'a woman' or 'a man'. Because the qualities identified as masculine were invariably given more value than those identified as feminine, women's inferiority to men was deeply ingrained within culture.

 CHECK THE BOOK
For further information on the sex/gender distinction, see *Gender Studies: Terms and Debates* (2003), edited by Anne Cranny-Francis, Wendy Waring, Pam Stavropoulos and Joan Kirby.

Arguments such as Rubin's demonstrate how, conventionally, 'gender' is made to follow on from 'sex' in an unproblematic way, so that it appears that women are gentle and nurturing *because* they are women; men are dominant and aggressive *because* they are men. Once alert to the possibility that such personality traits are acquired rather than inborn, feminists could argue that it was no more 'unnatural' for a woman to be dominant than a man, and that the ability to nurture could be equally expressed by men as by women.

These ideas are relevant to Margaretta Jolly's essay 'Towards a Masculine Maternal: Pat Barker's Bodily Fictions', in which she argues that Barker 'sets out to undo' the traditional gender binary in *Regeneration*, 'both fictionally and historically' (*Critical Perspectives on Pat Barker*, 2005, p. 247). It is this that leads to her depiction of what Jolly calls 'the masculine maternal' (p. 245). This positive concept, which exists as a counterbalance to the masculine

CONTEXT

Barker regards herself as a feminist, but does not see that as meaning that she should not write about men, arguing 'I never thought for a second that feminism is only about women' (quoted in Karin Westman, *Pat Barker's Regeneration: A Reader's Guide*, 2001, p. 14).

 CHECK THE NET

The online article 'Life in the Trenches' published on **www. firstworldwar. com** contains more details about trench routines. From the home page, click on 'Feature Articles' in the left-hand list, then scroll down to 'Life in the Trenches'.

ability to create war and destruction, is linked to the central theme of regeneration. Rivers becomes representative of the nurturing male, who regenerates his patients emotionally as well as psychologically. 'Fathering' does not adequately describe this process, as Rivers himself is well aware, although he questions throughout the novel 'how nurturing can become as deeply a masculine as well as a feminine identification' (p. 247); an attitude which demonstrates Rivers's reluctance to take on what he regards as a 'feminine' role.

In *Regeneration*, Barker depicts a consistent slippage between sex and gender that challenges traditional ways of viewing men's and women's roles. In wartime, men are meant to prove their masculinity in acts of violence and aggression, but have instead been reduced to '"feminine" passivity' (p. 108). In the trenches, the officers display a maternal care towards their men, and military duties resemble housekeeping within a macabre setting – cleaning up dead bodies, washing feet, making tea, checking food supplies and writing letters. In trying to perform their masculine roles, they end up performing female ones.

In contrast, women are depicted in the process of fulfilling active roles they were never before thought capable of. This makes it seem as if the sexes are exchanging places, as Billy Prior implies when he reflects that women seemed 'to have expanded in all kinds of ways, whereas men … had shrunk into a smaller and smaller space' (p. 90).

TRAUMA THEORY

Trauma theory employed within a literary context has two aims: 1) to study how texts represent traumatic events (such as war); and 2) to assess the extent to which they 'bear witness' to hidden or forgotten memories of trauma. The word 'trauma' refers to a horrific or shocking event which arouses great distress in the minds of those who have witnessed it. This can lead to repression – an attempt to forget what has happened in order to avoid the emotions of pain and fear aroused by remembering. This means that, as Cathy Caruth asserts in her study *Unclaimed Experience* (1996), 'trauma stands outside representation' (p. 17), since it cannot be properly spoken of or written about.

However, repression is only ever partial – because the traumatic event has not been fully accepted by and thus integrated within the conscious mind, fragmented recollections will persistently haunt the unconscious. If the individual refuses, or is unable, to 'move on', the traumatic event will remain ever present, in the form of flashbacks or neurotic behaviour. A resolution can only be achieved if the significant effects of the traumatic event are faced up to, spoken of and remembered.

Societies as well as individuals can be traumatised in this way – collective events such as the Holocaust and slavery are often written about in trauma theory. Trauma theorists would assert that trauma can be inherited, so even if somebody has not directly experienced the horror of Auschwitz or of slavery, he or she may still have to live with its effect upon the collective subconscious of his or her ethnic, racial or religious group. As Michelle Balaev argues in her essay 'Trends in Literary Trauma Theory' (2008), published in the journal *Mosaic* (41(12)), 'Traumatic experience is understood as a fixed and timeless photographic negative stored in an unlocatable place of the brain, but it maintains the ability to interrupt consciousness and maintains the ability to be transferred to non-traumatized individuals and groups'.

Literary texts thus play an important role in allowing trauma to be voiced, acting as part of the process whereby memories become assimilated and accepted, and hence robbed of their ability to haunt an individual or collective consciousness. Moreover, giving voice to trauma can be extremely important politically, by not allowing acts of persecution or genocide to be forgotten. The notion of 'bearing witness' is a significant aspect of trauma narratives, since it allows the evils of the past to be confronted, acknowledged and their consequences dealt with.

Many critical studies of Barker's work concentrate upon her representation of trauma. In his essay 'Pat Barker's *Regeneration* Trilogy: History and the Hauntological Imagination', published in the collection *Contemporary British Fiction* (2003), John Brannigan examines the motif of haunting in *Regeneration* and the other novels in the trilogy, observing that the text abounds in references

CHECK THE BOOK

A key text in trauma studies is Anne Whitehead's study *Trauma Fiction* (2004).

CONTEXT

Through the atrocity of the Holocaust, Adolf Hitler attempted to systematically exterminate the Jewish population of Europe. During the Second World War, approximately six million Jews were killed, many in concentration camps, such as Auschwitz.

CHECK THE BOOK

Pat Barker's daughter, Anna Ralph, published her first novel *The Floating Island* in 2007. Interviewed by the *Newcastle Journal* in May 2007, she said that she and her mother share an interest in 'trauma and memory'.

to ghosts and uncanny doublings, such as Sassoon's visions of dead comrades, and the phantom tastes and smells which prevent Burns from eating. The manifestations of such 'unreal' sights and sensations disrupt uncomplicated notions of time and rationality. For Brannigan, Barker's representation of the First World War centres upon its traumatic effects in both individual and social contexts – it 'repeats the time of other wars, churns up the dead of other centuries, and refuses to be contained in its present time' (p. 23). In his role as therapist, Rivers plays a pivotal role in helping his patients out of their haunted states, 'by encouraging them to put their repressed experiences into perspective and to recover absent, traumatic memories through introspection' (pp. 17–18). Brannigan argues, however, that the disorientating effects of the First World War linger in contemporary history, which remains in a traumatic condition, 'continually haunted by the memory of loss, and … constantly striving to regenerate the past' (p. 24).

MARXISM

Marxist literary theory, as its name suggests, uses the political theories of the nineteenth-century revolutionary philosopher Karl Marx to examine social and economic representations within literary texts. A key concern in Marxist thought is the concept of ideology, a set of principles, aims and beliefs that have been formulated to defend and promote the interests of a dominant social group. Ideology is, by its very nature, invisible; disseminated through every facet of the social order – the media, the family, the church, the legal system and so on – it defines a viewpoint that is accepted as the 'natural' order of things. A Marxist would argue that what is mistaken for free will is in fact the effects of ideology, which coerce people into 'voluntarily' maintaining a capitalist order in which wealth is produced by the many for the few. Marxists seek to uncover and deconstruct capitalist ideology in order to enable the creation of a more equal, classless society in which wealth is shared equally among all its members.

CONTEXT

Karl Marx (1818–83) was a German intellectual who is best known as the author of *The Communist Manifesto* (1848), in which he argued that the victory of socialism over capitalism was inevitable, aided by revolutionary action organised by the working class, or 'proletariat'.

Marxist literary theorists focus on a work's presentation of class and the social order, as well as the historical and economic circumstances surrounding its production. They might also be concerned with the social class of the author, examining the extent to which the author's own class-based assumptions have influenced his or her depiction of social relations within the text. The view that the novel form itself is innately middle class has been proposed by the critic Ian Watt in his influential study *The Rise of the Novel* (1957), which argues that the development of the novel in the eighteenth century is linked to the expanding influence of the middle classes, or bourgeoisie. With its focus upon the experiences of a specific character within a detailed world we are encouraged to see as a reflection of reality, the novel 'purports to be an authentic account of the actual experiences of individuals' (p. 27) who have the ability to improve their social status through their actions.

A Marxist reading of *Regeneration* would study Barker's depiction of class relations in Britain in the First World War, and note the discrepancy between the social status of most of her major characters, and her own. In the world inhabited by Rivers and Sassoon, class differentiations are ingrained and unalterable, and neither of them recognise the assumptions they are constantly making on the basis of these distinctions. The two men bond in the environs of the local Conservative Club, and Rivers arranges Sassoon's appointments around his golfing commitments. Yet Barker clearly does not identify with this kind of upper-middle-class perspective, from which she is separated by both time and personal background. Many of the class assumptions of the time seem archaic to us now; moreover, Barker, whose origins are firmly working class, could not be expected to feel much sympathy for such opinions.

Billy Prior and Sarah Lumb are both used by Barker as a means of critiquing the viewpoints of the more privileged characters in the novel and acting as indications of the social changes that the war was in the process of accelerating. A working-class officer and a working woman, both are figures in the process of transition. Prior is particularly significant in this regard, as he is able to comment on both the working and the upper classes. He is anxious to reject his working-class roots, yet he is also highly derogatory towards those who believe themselves to be his social superiors. He is also useful in acting as a focus for the highlighting of the unconscious prejudices of otherwise sympathetic characters such as Rivers –

> **CONTEXT**
>
> A particularly influential figure in the development of Marxist literary criticism is the French theorist Louis Althusser (1918–90). His concept of 'interpellation' describes the process whereby capitalism persuades its subjects that they are acting of their own free will when in reality the choices available to them are more limited than they realise.

Barker has said that he was introduced into the novel precisely 'to get up Rivers's nose' (quoted in Francis Spufford, 'Exploding the Myths: An Interview with Booker Prize-Winner Pat Barker', *Guardian Supplement*, 9 November 1995, p. 3).

CHECK THE FILM

In 1990, *Union Street* was made into a Hollywood film entitled *Stanley and Iris*, starring Robert De Niro and Jane Fonda. The film bears little relationship to the book – in Donna Perry's interview with Barker, her husband David commented that only 'about 2 per cent of the movie comes from the book' (*Backtalk*, 2003, p. 57).

Although most studies of *Regeneration* discuss Barker's presentation of class, the criticism of her work most strongly influenced by a Marxist viewpoint does not deal with this novel precisely, but with earlier works such as *Union Street*. In their essay 'From the East End to *EastEnders*: Representations of the Working Class, 1890–1990', Kathryn Dodd and Philip Dodd are very critical of the notion that *Union Street* depicts the working classes differently because of the working-class origins of its author; it is, they argue, 'still very much *about* the working class, not of it' (*Come On Down? Popular Media Culture in Post-War Britain*, 1992, p. 122). Similarly, Ian Hayward argues that Barker's focus on 'the interiority of women's experience' (*Working-Class Fiction*, 1997, p. 145) means that the narrative does not have a sufficiently detailed historical context. This means that 'it is difficult to date the action precisely, or to locate the influence of regionalism on the lives of these women' (p. 145).

PART FIVE

BACKGROUND

PAT BARKER'S LIFE AND WORKS

Pat Barker was born on 8 May 1943 in Thornaby-on-Tees, a town near Middlesbrough in the northeast of England. She never knew her father, and was brought up by her mother, Moyra, in the home of her grandmother and step-grandfather, who worked as a slaughterman. Barker grew up thinking that her father was an RAF pilot who had been killed in the Second World War, and it was only just before her mother died in 2000 that she found out that Moyra did not actually know his identity, having become pregnant while serving as a Wren in Dunfermline in Scotland.

When Barker was seven, her mother married and left Barker living with her grandparents. She was educated at the local grammar school, and her grandmother encouraged her to become a teacher. Barker herself had decided she wanted to be a writer by the time she was eight, and was eleven when she wrote her first novel, but her grandmother discouraged her, telling her that there was 'no money in it' (Donna Perry, *Backtalk*, 1993, p. 48). Instead, Barker went to the London School of Economics in 1962 to study history, then did teacher-training at Neville's Cross College in Durham, going on to teach history and government in colleges of further education.

Barker met her husband David, a Professor of Zoology at Durham University, in 1969 while teaching in Middlesbrough. She gave up teaching after the birth of their two children, John and Annabel, and instead began to write in earnest. Her husband supported her, taking care of the children while she worked, and in one incident, retrieving an early manuscript of what would become her first novel, *Union Street*, from the bin.

Barker has said that one of the reasons she did not begin to publish until the age of thirty-nine was that she lacked artistic role models. The only writers of working-class life she could find were male, and in their writing 'the women characters were very dead, one-

> **CONTEXT**
>
> The Women's Royal Navy Service, or Wrens, was founded in 1917. Disbanded in 1919, it was reformed in 1939 at the outbreak of the Second World War. Women worked as clerks, cooks, drivers and radar and communications operators.

dimensional' (Maya Jaggi, 'Dispatches from the Front', *Guardian*, 16 August 2003). Consequently, she kept trying to write 'slim, sensitive lady's novels' (Debbie Taylor, 'Pat Barker', *Mslexia* 5, Spring/Summer 2000), which did not allow her, she said, to express the 'earthiness and bawdiness in my voice' (Jaggi). The turning point for Barker came in 1978, when she attended a writing course at Lumb Bank in Yorkshire at which she met the writer Angela Carter. Carter read the manuscript of *Union Street* and encouraged her to send it to Virago Press for publication. When it was published in 1982, it was an instant success, becoming joint winner of the Fawcett Society Book Prize. The following year, the literary magazine *Granta* included Barker on their list of the twenty Best Young British Novelists. In 1984, she published *Blow Your House Down*, and *The Century's Daughter* (now published under the title *Liza's England*) appeared in 1986.

Together, these three novels established Barker's reputation as a writer of working-class **realism** with a feminist bent. *Union Street* focuses on the everyday lives of a poor community in the northeast of England, while *Blow Your House Down* tells the story of a group of prostitutes who are being stalked by a serial killer. *The Century's Daughter* centres upon the reminiscences of an old woman who has lived through the twentieth century and both world wars.

Barker's following novel, *The Man Who Wasn't There*, published in 1988, marked the growth of her interest in masculinity and paternity. Although there had always been a place for men in her novels – in *The Century's Daughter*, for example, the narrative voice is shared between that of Liza and her male social worker – this was the first book wholly centred upon a male character. The story of Colin, who fantasises about the father he has never known, introduces themes that were to become central to *Regeneration*, published three years later.

Pat Barker told Donna Perry in 1993 that the idea for *Regeneration* came from 'several channels' (*Backtalk*, p. 51). She was familiar with the poetry of Sassoon and Owen, and said that her first attempt at writing as a child was 'a terribly bad poem about the first world war when I was eleven' (pp. 51–2). In her twenties, reading Rivers's

CONTEXT

Blow Your House Down recalls the case of the Yorkshire Ripper, a man named Peter Sutcliffe who murdered thirteen women, many of them prostitutes, across the north of England between 1975 and 1981.

book *Conflict and Dream* provoked her interest further. Another major influence on the formation of *Regeneration* came from a more personal source. Her grandfather had volunteered to fight in the trenches when he was fifteen, and had been bayoneted on the battlefield. When Barker was a little girl she was fascinated by his battle scar, and he would allow her to stick her finger into the large indentation in his side. It was from him that she gained an impression of the horror of the soldiers' experiences: she told Donna Perry that he only began to speak about the war 'towards the end of his life because they [his memories] were so horrific that he didn't want to tell them before then' (p. 47).

Barker has said that 'of all my books, I'm fondest of *Regeneration*' (interview on the Penguin website), and certainly the success of this novel established her reputation as one of the best British novelists of the nineties. The two sequels to *Regeneration*, *The Eye in the Door* (1993) and *The Ghost Road* (1995) were also well received: *The Ghost Road* received the 1995 Booker Prize, and in 1996 Barker won the Author of the Year Prize from the Bookseller's Association. Barker has always said that she did not write *Regeneration* with the idea that it would be the first book in a trilogy, but that the subject-matter came to demand it. In an interview with Sheryl Stevenson, published in 2005 in the essay collection *Critical Perspectives on Pat Barker*, Barker said that she 'wrote and rewrote the final chapter of *Regeneration*, trying to give the sense of completion, and in fact I couldn't make it complete because the story ends with the end of the war' (p. 175). She then decided to write one more book, which had an even more indeterminate ending, 'because you have Prior going back to the war with all his hang-ups and difficulties' (p. 176). *The Ghost Road* follows the trilogy's main characters – Rivers, Prior and Owen – through to the end of the war, and reveals their fates.

Since the publication of the trilogy, Barker has remained primarily identified as a writer of contemporary novels about war, an assessment which is not entirely accurate. In 1998, she published *Another World*, which, although set in contemporary Newcastle-upon-Tyne, features a hundred-year-old veteran of the Great War,

CHECK THE BOOK

In 2008, the last surviving veteran of the war in the trenches of the Western Front, Harry Patch, published his memoir *The Last Fighting Tommy*. He is said not have spoken openly about his experiences until he turned one hundred.

CHECK THE NET

To find the interview with Penguin go to **www. penguin.co.uk**. Type 'border crossing' into the search box, click on the novel, then 'interview' on the left hand side. A radio interview with Barker on the publication of *Regeneration* can be found on the CBC Digital Archives website at **http://archives. cbc.ca**. Type 'Pat Barker' into the search box on the home page and follow the link.

Geordie, through whose recollections she continues to explore themes of trauma, memory and masculinity. *Border Crossing* and *Double Vision*, published in 2001 and 2003 respectively, do not return to the Great War for their subject matter, but nevertheless remain focused upon male protagonists caught up in traumatic situations. Barker has remarked that these two novels are linked to the trilogy insofar as they continue an ongoing interest in 'the theme of violence – the deep roots of violence and the links between criminal violence, domestic violence, and public violence' (*Critical Perspectives on Pat Barker*, 2005, p. 184).

However, Barker's most recent publication, *Life Class* (2007), is another period novel set between 1914 and 1918, telling the story of a group of students studying at the Slade School of Art in London when war breaks out. The main protagonist, Paul Tarrant, becomes a Red Cross volunteer at a field hospital behind the front lines in Belgium, which allows him to witness at first hand the terrible cost of the conflict. As in *Regeneration*, Barker mingles invented characters with those taken from real life, such as Professor Henry Tonks and Lady Ottoline Morell. But whereas the *Regeneration* trilogy explores trauma and its treatment, *Life Class* has taken up a more minor theme in the original novel, which is the ethics of representing the war in art. On the one hand, artists like Paul, who knows what the war is really like, have a responsibility to portray what they have seen; yet on the other, as Paul himself says, 'Nobody's going to hang that sort of thing in a gallery' (p. 175). It is a **paradox** that both recalls and develops the conversations between Owen and Sassoon in *Regeneration*, and continues Barker's ongoing interest in the representation of the Great War.

HISTORICAL BACKGROUND

THE FIRST WORLD WAR

The First World War was, in many people's eyes, the most catastrophic conflict of the twentieth century. It was the first 'world' war, in that it involved over one hundred countries from Europe, Africa, America, Asia and Australasia. This was because the

---

CONTEXT

Comparisons between the *Regeneration* trilogy and *Life Class* were inevitable: for example, Christopher Benfey in the *New York Times* observed that 'the novel covers some of the same ground – including battleground – as Barker's superb *Regeneration* Trilogy, with historical figures again mingling with invented ones and artists substituted for the poets Siegfried Sassoon and Wilfred Owen' (27 January 2008).

principal nations involved – Germany, Austria, Russia, France and Britain – were colonial powers, and drew the countries they governed into the conflict.

In addition, it was the first war to be fought as an industrial operation, due to the use of new technology. Tanks, gas and aeroplanes were all used in battle for the first time between 1914 and 1918. The mass production of weaponry such as machine guns and heavy artillery enabled killing to be done en masse, rather than through hand-to-hand fighting, and accounts for the devastating scale of the casualty figures. Great Britain and its Empire, for example, mobilised 8.9 million men in total during the course of the war, of which nearly a million were killed and two million wounded. For France the proportion was even greater – of over eight million sent to battle, over a million died, and over four million were wounded. In addition, Germany's use of airships, known as Zeppelins, on bombing raids over Britain meant that not even civilians were safe from the effects of war.

CHECK THE POEM
In his poem 'MCMXIV' (1964), Philip Larkin evokes the time before the outbreak of the First World War as a time of innocence that can never be recaptured.

The war was fought between two groups of countries: the Triple Entente, or Allies, composed of France, Britain, Russia and – later in the war – the United States; and the Central Powers, made up of Germany, Austro-Hungary and Turkey. Italy, allied with the Central Powers in the years leading up to the outbreak of war, delayed entry into the conflict until 1915, when it joined on the side of the Allies.

The event which sparked the conflict was the assassination of the Archduke Franz Ferdinand, heir to the throne of the Austrian Empire, and his wife Sophie, on a visit to the city of Sarajevo on 28 June 1914. The assassin was a member of a Serbian/Bosnian radical group, who wanted to free the rest of Serbia from Austrian control. However, the speed with which the war began indicated that the major European powers were already poised to fight. Rising tension between Germany and other European countries meant that they had been locked in an arms race from the beginning of the decade, and the systems of alliance that had been developed meant that any crisis would quickly escalate into all-out war.

THE FIRST WORLD WAR continued

CHECK THE BOOK

Cicely Hamilton's novel *William: An Englishman* (1918) emotively depicts the German invasion of Belgium.

The war was fought on a variety of fronts across the world, including the Eastern Front (Eastern Europe), the Middle Eastern Front and the Balkan Front (Serbia, Romania and Bulgaria). In addition, battles took place at sea and in the air. The British experience of the First World War, however, was predominantly (though not exclusively) centred upon the Western Front stretching across France and Belgium. Germany invaded Belgium on 1 August 1914, barely a month after the assassination of the Archduke, with the aim of taking Paris and forcing France to surrender, then turning to the east in order to mount an offensive against Russia. It was an extremely ambitious plan, and its failure led to years of trench warfare.

The French and the British immediately rose to Belgium's defence, with Britain declaring war on Germany on 4 August. Britain's professional standing army formed the British Expeditionary Force (BEF), and were successful in helping the Belgians to slow the German advance. The German troops were then engaged by the French army at the Battle of the Marne (5–11 September), which brought them to a halt. Consequently, both sides dug in and began to move sideways in a bid to take control of the Channel Ports. By 1915, the trench system had been established, and remained more or less static until the end of the war. The front line in France alone contained around 6,250 miles of trench, and in total, the Allies commanded 12,000 miles of trench.

The men who fought on the Western Front, therefore, spent most of their time below ground. Sniping and shelling accounted for many casualties, and full-blown hand-to-hand engagement with the enemy was relatively rare. When offensives were mounted, they were fought over a few miles of ground, and for most of the four years of the war failed to achieve the decisive breakthrough both sides were seeking.

One of the most notorious battles of the war, the Battle of the Somme, has become emblematic of the huge loss of life sustained for little or no gain that characterised conflict on the Western Front. It began on 1 July 1916, following two weeks' intensive shelling of the German lines. Assuming that most of the enemy were dead, the

Allied troops attacked in broad daylight. Thousands of men across a twenty-five-mile front walked towards the German lines, only to be mown down by machine-gun fire from soldiers who had survived the bombardment by moving into deep dugouts below the main trenches. By the end of the day, the British army had suffered 60,000 casualties, and by the time the offensive ended in November, British and French losses combined totalled three-quarters of a million men. The Allies had advanced less than seven miles, and most of that was lost over subsequent months.

It was not until the spring of 1918, when Germany launched a series of offensives on the Western Front which left them weakened and demoralised, that the Allies – strengthened by the US entry into the war in 1917 – were able to break through their lines. An official cease-fire was declared on 11 November 1918, bringing an end to four years of war.

The First World War was not, of course, called that at the time – it was known as the Great War, the 'war to end all wars'. It was such a terrible event that it was believed that such a conflict would never be allowed to happen again. Tragically, the peace settlement known as the Treaty of Versailles, signed on 28 June 1919, directly contributed to the outbreak of a second World War only twenty years later. Germany had been forced to accept responsibility for the war, reduce the size of its army and give up many of its territories, and its discontent with these terms contributed to its willingness to support the nationalist Nazi Party's rise to power.

SHELL-SHOCK

The phenomenon of what came to be known as 'shell-shock' was first officially noted in 1915 by the Cambridge psychologist Dr Charles Myers. He coined the term because he assumed that the cases of mutism and paralysis he had observed in soldiers were due to the physical or chemical effects of shells bursting at close range, and causing neurological disruption to the brain. But as the war continued, and cases began to mount, it became obvious that shell-shock, even while it might manifest itself in physical symptoms, was psychological in origin.

 CHECK THE NET
Extracts from the 1916 film *The Battle of the Somme*, which includes some actual battlefield footage, can be viewed on the website of the Imperial War Museum, at **http://collections. iwm.org.uk**. Type 'Somme' into the search box on the home page.

Although debates raged at the time about its exact causes – it was said to be no more than simple cowardice, hypochondria, the consequence of poor discipline or the manifestation of inherited weakness – psychologists and doctors began to see it as a response to the peculiar tensions of trench warfare, a conclusion supported by the fact that it was a phenomenon almost wholly confined to the Western Front. Shell-shock reached endemic proportions in the trenches: by 1916, it was thought that as many as forty per cent of war casualties were due to shell-shock, and it accounted for one-seventh of all medical discharges from the army. In response, the army moved to set up treatment centres all over the United Kingdom – by 1918, six specialist shell-shock hospitals for officers and thirteen for enlisted men had been established in the country.

> **CONTEXT**
>
> 'In the year ending 30 April 1917, while the ratio of officers to men at the Front was 1:30 and of wounded officers to men 1:24, the ratio of officers to men in hospitals for war neurasthenics was 1:6' (Joanna Bourke, *Dismembering the Male: Men's Bodies, Britain and the Great War*, 1999, p. 112).

One of the aspects of shell-shock that the military authorities found hardest to comprehend was that officers, who were members of the social elite, were four times more likely to break down than ordinary soldiers. This was truly disturbing in a society divided by rigorous class distinctions, in which the upper classes were generally regarded as innately stronger and more intelligent than members of the working classes. However, the responsibilities placed on officers' shoulders – many of them, particularly in the latter part of the war, barely out of public school – were enormous. Junior officers were expected to lead from the front and by example, serving as role models of masculine courage and fortitude to their men. Indeed, it was noted by psychiatrists that it was often the officers deemed most courageous and with a reputation for risk-taking who were most vulnerable to breakdown.

Another distinction that emerged between ordinary soldiers and officers was that they tended to present with different symptoms. Men in the ranks usually manifested signs of shell-shock that included paralysis, dumbness, bodily contortions and uncontrollable twitches, while officers suffered from nightmares, stammering and hallucinations. Psychologists such as W. H. R. Rivers argued in *Instinct and the Unconscious*, published in 1922, that this was due to the fact that the more highly educated officer 'has a more complex and varied' mental life, while the private soldier, because of his 'simpler mental training', is more likely 'to be content with the crude solution of the conflict between instinct and duty which is provided by disabilities such as dumbness or the helplessness of a limb'. Consequently, it was customary to diagnose officers as 'neurasthenic', while private soldiers were, more bluntly, termed 'hysterics'.

This in turn led to the development of two different regimes for the treatment of shell-shock. Officers were often subject to a more benign psychological regime, involving hypnosis, the 'talking cure' (psychoanalysis) and beneficial physical activity. Private soldiers, in contrast, were more likely to be treated in ways that resembled punishment, including electric-shock treatment and vigorous, often painful, massage.

In all cases, shell-shock was regarded as having compromised the masculinity of those who suffered from it. The word 'hysteria' comes from the Greek 'hystera', or 'womb', indicating the extent to which it was a complaint traditionally associated with women. Until the First World War, the majority of patients treated for hysteria were female, which meant that men who broke down were invariably seen as feminised. In *The Female Malady*, Elaine Showalter argues that the belief that shell-shock represented 'a feminine kind of behaviour in male subjects' was 'a recurrent theme in the discussions of war neuroses. When military doctors and psychiatrists dismissed shell-shock patients as cowards, they were often hinting at effeminacy or homosexuality' (1987, p. 172).

CHECK THE POEM

In 'The Immortals', Isaac Rosenberg (1890–1918) depicts the battle against war trauma as a nightmarish and never-ending fight against the Devil.

WOMEN'S WAR WORK

The First World War was a momentous event in women's history because it marked the first time that British women were able to serve the war effort in a recognised capacity. As Nosheen Khan writes in her book *Women's Poetry of the First World War*:

> Since the beginning of history women have been mixed up in war, but until the conflict of 1914–18 war presented no direct challenge to them. Prior to that time they might have deplored war's savagery, pitied its victims, honoured the courage of its heroes and felt gratitude for the protection which the army offered them, yet they remained spectators. War was by tradition

alien to women, it was not their province. The First World War changed this; it provided women with an opportunity to participate in and observe war on a scale hitherto unknown. (1988, p. 106)

Women's contributions were wide ranging, from taking over the jobs left vacant when men left to enlist, to joining one of the many semimilitary organisations that had been set up before or at the outbreak of war, such as the Women's Hospital Corps, the Women's Land Army, the Women's Auxiliary Army Corps (WAAC) or the Voluntary Aid Detachment (VAD).

The VAD, initially established in 1909, became one of the pivotal organisations of the First World War, training thousands of women as assistant nurses, ambulance drivers and cooks. From 1915, VADs were allowed to serve at the front, which meant that women over the age of twenty-three with more than three months' experience were able to travel to the Western Front, Mesopotamia, Gallipoli and the Eastern Front, where they worked as nurses, ambulance drivers and clerks. By 1916, the VAD organisation had recruited 80,000 members, the majority of them upper- and middle-class women.

The women who went to work in British munitions factories, in contrast, were mainly working class; many, like Sarah Lumb, had formerly worked in domestic service. By the end of the war, nearly a million women were working in British munitions factories, drawn there by both a desire to serve the war effort and the relatively high wages (although women still earned only fifty per cent of the wage given to male munitions workers).

Munitions work was hard, dirty and often dangerous. Because it was a job that required no skill or prior experience, women were mainly employed to fill shell casings with TNT. This meant that they were labouring in very risky conditions indeed: in *Nice Girls and Rude Girls: Women Workers in World War I* (2000), Deborah Thom notes that the Woolwich Arsenal, the largest munitions factory in Britain, was comprised of '172 buildings, each with a ton or more of explosive in an area of three square miles' (p. 151).

CHECK THE BOOK

Not So Quiet by Helen Zenna Smith (1930) describes the experiences of a group of female ambulance drivers behind the front lines in France.

QUESTION

Why do you think Barker chooses to write about female munitions workers, yet keeps the VAD nurses in the background of her novel?

In addition, all workers were affected to some degree by TNT poisoning, which caused a variety of symptoms, including headaches, eczema, shortness of breath and heart palpitations, and in some extreme cases workers died from the toxic effects of the explosive. All those who worked with TNT had yellow-stained skin and hair, which led to their popular nickname of 'canaries'.

In many ways, the role played by munitions workers was more controversial than that of 'caring' organisations like the VAD because their job involved the production of weaponry. Thus, rather than trying to preserve life, they were directly involved in the business of taking it, which was regarded as rather problematic in a society that saw women as the 'gentler' sex.

> **CONTEXT**
>
> A popular song of the First World War, 'The Rose that Grows in No-Man's Land', demonstrates the romanticism attached to the figure of the nurse, who is described as 'the one red rose the soldier knows'.

LITERARY BACKGROUND

LITERATURE OF THE FIRST WORLD WAR

The First World War was not only fought by professional soldiers. On the outbreak of the conflict, thousands of British men volunteered for military service in response to the call from the Secretary of State for War, Field Marshall Kitchener. After the passing of the Military Service Act in 1916, these volunteers were supplemented by conscripts, when war service became compulsory for all fit men between the ages of eighteen and forty-one.

This led to a large number of highly literate, educated men gaining first-hand experience of warfare, which they expressed through the writing of poetry, memoirs and novels published both during and after the war. In his study *Fiction of the First World War* (1988), George Parfitt observes that 'No earlier war … gave rise to an equivalent body of writing and, for the first time, there was the possibility of a substantial literature produced by combatants, for the armies of the Great War were the first literate British armies' (p. 135). The principal literary figures of the First World War were from the officer class – public school educated and well read in classical literature and the work of British writers such as Shakespeare, Milton and the Romantic poets.

The first literary form that emerged following the outbreak of war was poetry; although its form and content was to change drastically over the course of the conflict. Early First World War poetry tended to be patriotic in sentiment and **pastoral** in form, as exemplified in the verse of Rupert Brooke. Siegfried Sassoon and Wilfred Owen, however, represent a very different way of writing about the war in verse. Both began as poets in the pastoral tradition, but their experiences changed their poetic intentions and the forms they used to express them. Sassoon's poetry began to represent in angrily realistic terms the suffering he saw around him on the front line, and – as *Regeneration* shows – he also taught Owen to do the same. Descriptions of rural scenes give way to depictions of the battlefield, and poetic language is rejected for something harsher and more **idiomatic**. In a famous statement, Owen goes so far as to suggest that poetic style must be rejected when writing about war in order to allow the subject matter to speak for itself: 'Above all, I am not concerned with Poetry. My subject is War, and the pity of War. The poetry is in the Pity'.

Novels and memoirs about the war written by combatants were slower to emerge, possibly because, while it is possible to compose short verses while on active service, it is a good deal harder to embark on a sustained piece of prose writing. It was not until 1928 – a full ten years after the end of the war – that memoirs and novels began to emerge in any number. This was partly due to the fact that such publications were becoming marketable, but it was also as if the men who had experienced the horrors of warfare needed time in which to process memories that continued to traumatise them. The first volume of Siegfried Sassoon's trilogy of memoirs, *Memoirs of a Fox-Hunting Man*, was published in 1928, the same year as Edmund Blunden's *Undertones of War*, while Robert Graves published his memoir *Goodbye to All That* in 1929. Graves wrote his book in only eight weeks, while still experiencing the after-effects of war trauma, including nightmares and twitching. Such texts demonstrate the thin line between fact and fiction characteristic of the writing of the First World War. Graves's memoir purports to be accurate, but uses many novelistic devices, while Sassoon's cloaks the facts in a thin veil of invention – he changes, for example, the names of most of the characters and places in the **narrative**.

Women's contribution to the literary output of the Great War has customarily been overlooked, although since the 1980s there has been a sustained effort to recover and reconsider it. Whether their writing can be classified as 'war literature' in the strictest sense is debatable, if we restrict the term to describe writing by combatants. Catherine Reilly's anthology of women's poetry of the First World War, *Scars Upon My Heart* (1981), contains nothing like the poetry of Owen and Sassoon, but the verses anthologised within it do convey the variety of female responses to the conflict, ranging from poems written by VAD nurses to verses of mourning and loss. Women produced war memoirs, too – most notably, Vera Brittain's *Testament of Youth*, published in 1933. Brittain served as a VAD nurse during the war in London, France and Malta, and her text records her experiences, as well as memorialising the men – her fiancé, her brother and her two best friends – she lost between 1914 and 1918. Although women's writing of the First World War can never be the literary response of a combatant, all women wrote from direct experience, either as war workers or as worried, grieving wives, mothers and girlfriends.

The First World War gave rise to a number of literary stereotypes through which writers could address the continuing memory of the conflict in the years after 1918, the most prevalent of which was the figure of the shell-shocked soldier. In Rebecca West's novel *The Return of the Soldier*, published in 1918, the impact of shell-shock on families is explored in the story of Chris Baldry, who is sent home from the front with amnesia. Virginia Woolf, too, wrote about shell-shock in *Mrs Dalloway* (1925), which features the **tragic** character of Septimus Warren Smith, who is so traumatised that he cannot adapt to a peacetime existence. R. C. Sherriff's play *Journey's End*, first performed in 1928, is set entirely in an officers' dugout in a trench in the final months of the war, and depicts the struggle of its characters to ward off mental collapse.

REPRESENTING THE FIRST WORLD WAR IN CONTEMPORARY FICTION

The First World War has taken on the status of a myth in contemporary society. To term it in this way is not to imply that the Great War did not happen, as it is an indisputable historical event.

CONTEXT

The large number of publications about the War from the late 1920s onwards sparked what has become known as 'the War Books Controversy', when readers and critics expressed horror at the negative depictions of war by such writers as Graves, Blunden and Sassoon.

CONTEXT

As a result of her experiences during the First World War, Vera Brittain became a life-long pacifist, and was an ardent supporter of the League of Nations Union.

REPRESENTING THE FIRST WORLD WAR IN CONTEMPORARY FICTION continued

**CHECK
THE POEM**

An eloquent poet of the Gulf War is Tony Harrison, whose poem 'A Cold Coming' (1991) was inspired by a photograph of the charred body of an Iraqi soldier inside a burnt-out truck. More recently, he has written about the 2003 invasion of Iraq in poems such as 'Baghdad Lullaby' and 'Iraquatrains' (2003).

**CHECK
THE BOOK**

For literary responses to the 9/11 attacks and their aftermath, including the London bombings of 7 July 2005, see Jonathan Safran Foer's *Incredibly Loud and Incredibly Close* (2005), Ian McEwan's *Saturday* (2005) and *Falling Man* by Don DeLillo (2007).

Instead, the use of the word 'myth' signifies that the war has virtually passed out of the realm of lived experience, and can now only be remembered through narratives passed down to us from those directly involved in it. In the twenty-first century, almost all of those who can remember it first hand are now dead, and for us it is an event we learn about through history lessons, stories, documentaries, museum exhibitions and commemorative occasions such as Remembrance Day. Novels such as *Regeneration* are one way in which the story of the First World War is kept alive: as its readers we are the final link in a chain of transmission which begins with the actual event itself, then its translation into literary formats such as poetry, fiction and memoirs, followed by Barker's own reading of this material in the formation of her narrative.

As previously discussed in **Part One: Reading** *Regeneration*, the novel participated in a wider growth of interest in the First World War in Britain in the 1990s. This was, first, indicative of a general recognition that, with the number of survivors of the war dwindling, a conscious effort was going to have to be made to maintain remembrance of a conflict that had shaped the course of twentieth-century history. Second, world events in the nineties, particularly the Gulf War, had sharpened public consciousness of the failure of the First World War to be 'the war to end all wars'.

In terms of scale, the Gulf War was not in any way comparable to the First World War. Nevertheless, it led to the mobilisation of British troops and revived debates about the morality of warfare. And in comparison to the extremely technological nature of the Gulf War, with its use of computer-controlled, precisely targeted missiles, memories of the First World War evoked a kind of nostalgia (however misplaced) for what now seemed a more 'traditional' form of fighting. With the 9/11 attacks on New York's World Trade Center in 2000 and the US declaration of the 'War on Terror' resulting in a further invasion of Iraq and the overthrow of Saddam Hussein's regime, the First World War continues to act as literary subject matter for novelists who wish to examine the morality of warfare and the practice of commemoration.

This renewed awareness of international conflict may account for the remarkable number of contemporary novelists taking the First World War as their subject matter in the nineties and beyond, including Sebastian Faulks's *Birdsong* (1993), Robert Edric's *In Desolate Heaven* (1997) and *In Zodiac Light* (2008), *Nineteen Twenty-One* by Adam Thorpe (2001) and Ben Elton's *The First Casualty* (2005). Many take commemoration as their central theme – *Birdsong*, for example, is a narrative that intermingles the experiences of an officer, Stephen Wraysford, on the Western Front with the efforts of his granddaughter, Elizabeth, to decipher his encoded diaries in 1976. Through this device Faulks allows the past and the near present to comment **ironically** upon each other, emphasising both the necessity of remembering and our inability to recover everything, since Faulks does not allow Elizabeth to learn about all of the things that happen to Stephen in his sections of the novel. In this way, Faulks emphasises that contemporary representations of the First World War can never capture the reality experienced by those who lived through it, but can only ever produce partial and inadequate accounts of an event that will always evade representation.

CHECK THE BOOK

Robert Edric's novel *In Zodiac Light* depicts the postwar incarceration of the composer and poet Ivor Gurney in the City of London Mental Hospital, Dartford.

CHECK THE FILM

The 1999 film *The Trench* is one example of the way in which contemporary depictions of the Great War still employ many of the stereotypes developed by the writers who experienced the war.

World events	Author's life	Literary events
		1888 Birth of Siegfried Sassoon
		1893 Birth of Wilfred Owen
1914 (28 June) assassination of Archduke Franz Ferdinand; (28 July) Austria-Hungary declares war on Serbia; (1–4 August) Germany declares war on Russia and France, German troops enter Belgium; (4 August) Britain declares war on Germany; (6 August) National Union of Women's Suffrage Societies announces suspension of activities for the duration of the war; (10 August) British government releases all imprisoned suffragettes; (22–24 August) Battle of Mons; (3–9 September) First Battle of the Marne; (19 October–21 November) First Battle of Ypres		
1915 Restrictions against members of the Voluntary Aid Detachment (VADs) serving at the front lifted; women begin to be employed as munitions workers and in other jobs; (19 January) bombing of Yarmouth and King's Lynn, the first Zeppelin raid against Britain; (22 April–24 May) Second Battle of Ypres, Germans use gas for the first time; (25 September–15 October) Battle of Loos		**1915** (November) Sassoon meets Robert Graves

World events	Author's life	Literary events
1916 Formation of the Women's Royal Naval Service (Wrens) and the Women's Land Army; (February) conscription introduced for single men and childless widowers aged eighteen to forty-one; (21 February–18 December) Siege of Verdun; (25 May) Military Service Act establishes compulsory military service for all men aged between eighteen and forty-one; (1 July–13 November) Battle of the Somme; (5 December) Lloyd George succeeds Asquith as Prime Minister		
1917 House of Commons begins discussing the possibility of giving women the vote; (28 March) the Women's Auxiliary Army Corps (WAAC) established; (6 April) United States of America enters the war; (9 April–16 May) Battle of Arras; (7–14 June) Battle of Messines; (31 July–6 November) Third Battle of Ypres (Passchendaele); (15 December) Russia and Germany sign peace treaty		**1917** (June) Owen arrives at Craiglockhart; (July) Sassoon arrives at Craiglockhart; (August) Sassoon and Owen meet; publication of Sassoon's first collection of poems, *The Old Huntsman*
1918 British bombing raids against Germany begin; (21 March–5 April) Germans launch the Ludendorff Offensive;		**1918** (4 November) Owen killed in action; Siegfried Sassoon, *Counter-Attack*; Rebecca West, *Return of the Soldier*

World events	Author's life	Literary events
1918 cont. (28 March) House of Commons votes to enfranchise women over the age of thirty who are householders, the wives of householders, occupiers of a property worth an annual rent of £5 or more and university graduates; (1 April) The Royal Air Force (RAF) and Women's Royal Air Force (WRAF) formed; (27 May–2 June) Third Battle of the Aisne; (15 July– 5 August) Second Battle of the Marne; (8 August– 3 September) Battle of Amiens; (27 September– 11 November) Battle of Cambrai-St-Quentin; (30 September) Bulgaria signs an armistice; (30 October) Turkey signs an armistice; (3 November) Austria-Hungary signs an armistice; (11 November) Germany signs an armistice		
1919 (18 January) Paris Peace Conference; (28 June) signing of the Treaty of Versailles		**1919** Seven of Owen's war poems published in *Wheels*, a literary magazine edited by Edith Sitwell
		1920 *Poems of Wilfred Owen* published, co-edited by Siegfried Sassoon and Edith Sitwell, with an introduction by Siegfried Sassoon
1921 (11 November) Royal British Legion launches the first Poppy Day		
		1925 Virginia Woolf, *Mrs Dalloway*

World events	Author's life	Literary events
		1928 Siegfried Sassoon, *Memoirs of a Fox-Hunting Man*; R. C. Sherriff, *Journey's End*; Edmund Blunden, *Undertones of War*
		1929 Robert Graves, *Goodbye to All That*; Erich Maria Remarque, *Im Westen nichts Neues (All Quiet on the Western Front)*; Fredric Manning, *The Middle Parts of Fortune*; Mary Borden, *The Forbidden Zone*
		1930 Siegfried Sassoon, *Memoirs of an Infantry Officer*; Helen Zenna Smith, *Not So Quiet*
		1931 *The Poems of Wilfred Owen*, edited by Edmund Blunden
		1933 Vera Brittain, *Testament of Youth*
1936–9 Spanish Civil War		**1936** Siegfried Sassoon, *Sherston's Progress*
1939–45 Second World War		
	1943 (8 May) Born in Thornaby-on-Tees, near Middlesbrough	
	1954 Attends King James Grammar School, Knaresborough	
	1955 Attends Grangefield Grammar School, Stockton-on-Tees	
1959–75 Vietnam War		

World events	Author's life	Literary events
	1962–5 Reads International History at London School of Economics	**1962** First performance of Benjamin Brittain's choral work, *War Requiem*, which includes musical adaptations of Wilfred Owen's poems
		1963 *The Collected Poems of Wilfred Owen*, edited by C. Day Lewis; staging of *Oh, What a Lovely War!* by Joan Littlewood and the Theatre Workshop; A. J. P. Taylor, *The First World War: An Illustrated History*
		1964 BBC1 screens *The Great War*, a documentary series commemorating the fiftieth anniversary of the outbreak of the First World War; publication of *Up the Line to Death: War Poets 1914–18*, edited by Brian Gardner
1965 Winston Churchill dies	**1965–6** Studies for Diploma of Education, Durham University	
	1969 Meets David Barker, Professor of Zoology at Durham University	**1969** Release of the film version of *Oh! What a Lovely War*, directed by Richard Attenborough
	1970 Son John born	
		1971 Publication of Susan Hill's *Strange Meeting*, a novel set in the First World War inspired by Owen's poem of the same title
	1974 Daughter Annabel born	**1974** Jennifer Johnston, *How Many Miles to Babylon?*

World events	Author's life	Literary events
		1975 Paul Fussell, *The Great War and Modern Memory*
	1978 Marries David Barker; attends writing course at Lumb Bank in Yorkshire and is mentored by Angela Carter	**1978** Eric Leed, *No Man's Land: Combat and Identity in World War I*
		1979 BBC screens an adaptation of Vera Brittain's *Testament of Youth*
	1982 *Union Street* published by Virago Press; the novel becomes joint winner of the Fawcett Society Book Prize	
	1983 Included in the Book Marketing Council's list of Twenty Best Young British Novelists	
	1984 *Blow Your House Down* published	
		1985 Elaine Showalter, *The Female Malady*
	1986 *The Century's Daughter* (*Liza's England*) published	
		1989 BBC screens the comedy series *Blackadder Goes Forth*. The final episode, in which the characters go 'over the top' to certain death, was broadcast a week before Remembrance Day
	1988 *The Man Who Wasn't There* published	
1990 (2 August) Iraqi invasion of Kuwait; (7 August) Operation Desert Shield implemented when US troops move into Saudi Arabia	**1990** Release of *Stanley and Iris*, a Hollywood film adaptation of *Union Street* starring Jane Fonda and Robert De Niro	

World events	Author's life	Literary events
1991 (16 January) Operation Desert Storm begins: the United States, supported by the United Nations, launch air campaign against Iraq; (24 February) ground troops engage with the Iraqi invasion force in Kuwait and enter Iraq; Iraqi troops retreat; (April 6) President Bush (Snr) declares a cease-fire	**1991** *Regeneration* published	**1991** Tony Harrison, *A Cold Coming*
	1992 American edition of *Regeneration* chosen as one of the four best novels of the year by the editors of the *New York Times Book Review*	
1993 First al-Qaeda attack on the World Trade Center in New York using a car bomb: six people killed	**1993** *The Eye in the Door* published; awarded the Guardian Prize for Fiction; Barker receives the degree of Honorary MLitt from the University of Teeside	**1993** Sebastian Faulks, *Birdsong*
	1995 *The Ghost Road* published; awarded the Booker Prize for Fiction	
	1996 Publication of a single-volume edition of the *Regeneration* trilogy by Viking; Barker awarded Author of the Year Prize by the Bookseller's Association and the degree of Honorary DLitt by Napier University; (14 May) Barker presents a BBC2 documentary, *On the Ghost Road*, about a tour of the French battlefields; Virago reissue her first three novels in the 'Modern Classics' series	

World events

2001 (11 September) al-Qaeda attack the World Trade Center in New York using hijacked aircraft, two other aircraft also hijacked and crashed, a total of 2,974 people killed; America declare the launch of the War on Terror, and invade Afganistan

2003 (March) American invasion of Iraq, supported by troops from Britain, Australia, Poland and Denmark; (April) Baghdad taken; (December) Saddam Hussein captured

Author's life

1997 *Regeneration* (US title *Behind the Lines*) made into a film directed by Gillies MacKinnon, starring Jonathan Pryce, Jonny Lee Miller and James Wilby; Barker becomes an Honorary Fellow of the London School of Economics; awarded Honorary PhD by the Open University and the University of Hertfordshire

1998 *Another World* published

1999 Awarded a CBE (Commander of the British Empire) in the Queen's New Year's Honours List

2001 *Border Crossing* published

2003 *Double Vision* published

2007 *Life Class* published

Literary events

1997 BBC screens *1914–18: The Great War and the Shaping of the Twentieth Century*; Spice Girls publicise the Poppy Appeal

1998 David Hartnett, *Brother to Dragons*

1999 *The Trench*, directed by William Boyd

2001 Adam Thorpe, *Nineteen Twenty-One*

2008 Robert Edric, *In Zodiac Light*

PROSE FICTION

Pat Barker, *The Eye in the Door* (1993)

Pat Barker, *The Ghost Road* (1995)

Pat Barker, *Life Class* (2007)

Sebastian Barry, *A Long, Long Way* (2005)

Robert Edric, *In Desolate Heaven* (1997)

Robert Edric, *In Zodiac Light* (2008)

Ben Elton, *The First Casualty* (2005)

Sebastian Faulks, *Birdsong* (1993)

Ford Maddox Ford, *Parade's End* (1924–8)

Cicely Hamilton, *William – An Englishman* (1918)

David Hartnett, *Brother to Dragons* (1998)

Mark Helprin, *A Soldier of the Great War* (1991)

Ernest Hemingway, *A Farewell to Arms* (1929)

Susan Hill, *Strange Meeting* (1971)

Jennifer Johnston, *How Many Miles to Babylon?* (1974)

Fredric Manning, *Her Privates We* (1930)

Irene Rathbone, *We That Were Young* (1932)

Helen Zenna Smith, *Not So Quiet* (1930)

Adam Thorpe, *Nineteen Twenty-One* (2001)

Rebecca West, *The Return of the Soldier* (1918)

Virginia Woolf, *Jacob's Room* (1921)

Virginia Woolf, *Mrs Dalloway* (1925)

PROSE NON-FICTION

MEMOIRS

Edmund Blunden, *Undertones of War* (Penguin, 1928)

Vera Brittain, *Testament of Youth* (Virago, 1933)

Robert Graves, *Goodbye to All That* (Penguin, 1929)

Siegfried Sassoon, *The Complete Memoirs of George Sherston* (one-volume edition of *Memoirs of a Fox-Hunting Man, Memoirs of an Infantry Officer* and *Sherston's Progress*) (Faber, 1937)

Siegfried Sassoon, *Siegfried's Journey 1916–1920* (Faber, 1945)

DIARIES, LETTERS AND BIOGRAPHY

Vera Brittain, ed. by Alan Bishop, *Chronicle of Youth: Great War Diary 1913–17* (Gollancz, 1981)

Alan Bishop and Mark Bostridge, eds, *Letters from a Lost Generation: First World War Letters of Vera Brittain and Four Friends* (Abacus, 1998)

Dominic Hibberd, *Wilfred Owen: A New Biography* (Weidenfield and Nicholson, 2002)

Wilfred Owen, *Wilfred Owen Collected Letters* (Oxford University Press, 1967)

Svetlana Palmer and Sarah Wallis, *A War in Words* (Pocket Books, 2003)

Richard Slobodin, *W.H.R. Rivers* (Columbia University Press, 1978)

Michael Walsh, *Brothers in War* (Ebury Press, 2006)

Jean Moorcroft Wilson, *Siegfried Sassoon: The Making of a War Poet* (Duckworth, 1998)

DRAMA

Alan Bleasedale, *The Monocled Mutineer* (Hutchinson, 1986)

Richard Curtis, Ben Elton *et al.*, *Blackadder Goes Forth* (included in *Blackadder: The Whole Damn Dynasty*) (Penguin, 1989)

Joan Littlewood, *Oh! What a Lovely War* (Methuen, 1965)

Stephen MacDonald, *Not About Heroes* (Faber, 1983)

Frank McGuinness, *Observe the Sons of Ulster Marching Towards the Somme* (Faber, 1986)

Miles Malleson, *Black 'ell* (1916)

Somerset Maugham, *For Services Rendered* (1932)

George Bernard Shaw, *O'Flaherty V.C.* (1915)

George Bernard Shaw, *Heartbreak House* (1919)

R. C. Sherriff, *Journey's End* (Heinemann, 1928)

Peter Whelan, *The Accrington Pals* (Methuen, 1982)

Nick Whitby, *To the Green Fields and Beyond* (Faber, 2000)

POETRY

Robert Giddings, *The War Poets* (Bloomsbury, 1988)

Daniel W. Hipp, *The Poetry of Shell Shock: Wartime Trauma and Healing in Wilfred Owen, Ivor Gurney and Siegfried Sassoon* (McFarland, 2005)

Christopher Martin, *War Poems* (Collins Educational, 1990)

Vivien Noakes, ed., *Voices of Silence: the Alternative Book of First World War Poetry* (Sutton, 2006)

Ian M. Parsons, *Men Who March Away* (Parsons, 1965)

Catherine Reilly, ed., *Scars Upon My Heart* (Virago, 1981)

Jon Silkin, ed., *The Penguin Book of First World War Poetry* (Penguin, 1985)

Jon Stallworthy, ed., *The Oxford Book of War Poetry* (Oxford, 1984)

Various, *The Wordsworth Book of First World War Poetry* (Wordsworth editions, 1995)

Various, *Poems of the Great War: 1914–1918* (Penguin, 1998)

HISTORY AND TESTIMONY

William Allison and John Fairley, *The Monocled Mutineer* (Quartet Books, 1978)

Max Arthur, ed., *Forgotten Voices* (Ebury Press, 2002)

Max Arthur, *Last Post* (Phoenix, 2005)

Corelli Barnett, *The Great War* (BBC, 1979)

Allyson Booth, *Postcards from the Trenches* (Oxford University Press, 1996)

Nigel Fountain, ed., *Women at War* (Michael O'Mara Books, 2002)

Richard Holmes, *Tommy* (Harper Perennial, 2005)

Eric Leed, *No Man's Land: Combat and Identity in World War I* (Cambridge University Press, 1979)

Lyn MacDonald, *Somme* (Penguin, 1983)

Ben MacIntyre, *A Foreign Field* (Harper Collins, 2001)

Harry Patch (with Richard Van Emden), *The Last Fighting Tommy* (Bloomsbury, 2008)

Dan Todman, *The Great War: Myth and Memory* (Hambledon Continuum, 2005)

Richard Van Emden, *The Trench: Experiencing Life on the Front Line, 1916* (Bantam, 2002)

Richard Van Emden, *Britain's Last Tommies: Final Memories from Soldiers of the 1914–18 War, in their Own Words* (Leo Cooper, 2005)

LITERARY CRITICISM AND CULTURAL COMMENTARY

Kate Adie, *Corsets to Camouflage: Women and War* (Coronet, 2003)
A very accessible survey by the former BBC war correspondent of women's involvement in war, from the First World War to the Gulf War

Adrian Barlow, *The Great War in British Literature* (Cambridge University Press, 2000)
A text aimed primarily at 'A' level students, which combines analysis of First World War writing with extracts and study activities. A good basic introduction

Bernard Berganzi, *Heroes' Twilight* (Constable, 1965; third edition, Carcanet Press, 1996)
An early, but still valuable, study, which examines the major poets and writers of 1914–18. The amended third edition has an extra final chapter, which also considers the mythologisation of the war in more recent contemporary fiction such as *Strange Meeting* and *Birdsong*

Paul Fussell, *The Great War and Modern Memory* (Oxford University Press, 1975)
One of the most important cultural studies of the Great War, which examines the part played by literature in the commemoration of the war in contemporary culture through an impressively wide-ranging, multidisciplinary context

Sharon Ouditt, *Fighting Forces, Writing Women* (Routledge, 1994)
A readable and wide-ranging study of women's participation in the First World War, which examines not only literature, but also magazines, memoirs and diaries

Ben Shephard, *A War of Nerves* (Pimlico, 2002)
This book examines the development of military psychology between 1914 and 1918, but the first twelve chapters discuss shell-shock and the First World War specifically. It contains valuable background information on Rivers's regime at Craiglockhart, but is rather dismissive of Barker's fictional representation

Claire M. Tylee, *The Great War and Women's Consciousness* (University of Iowa Press, 1990)
A text that played a pivotal role in the recovery of First World War writing by women, focusing mainly on memoirs and novels

allusion a passing reference in a work of literature to something outside the text; may include other works of literature, myth, historical facts or biographical detail

ambiguity the capacity of words and sentences to have double, multiple or uncertain meanings

canon group of literary works deemed to be 'great' because of their universal relevance and intellectual appeal

colloquial the everyday speech used by people in informal situations

couplet a pair of rhymed lines of any metre

dialect a regional variety of language distinguished by accent, grammar and vocabulary

discourse ways of conceptualising knowledge in language

elegiac sorrowful, mournful

flashback a scene inserted into the narrative that goes back in time in order to inform the reader of events that predate the start of the story

idiom a word or phrase specific to the language or culture from which it comes, which has a different meaning from what is expected

imagery descriptive language which uses images to make actions, objects and characters more vivid in the reader's mind. Metaphors and similes are examples of imagery

irony the humorous or sarcastic use of words to imply the opposite of what they normally mean; incongruity between what might be expected and what actually happens; the ill-timed arrival of an event that had been hoped for

metaphor a figure of speech in which a word or phrase is applied to an object, a character or an action which does not literally belong to it, in order to imply a resemblance and create an unusual or striking image in the reader's mind

metre the rhythmic arrangement of syllables in poetic verse

motif a recurring idea in a work, which is used to draw the reader's attention to a particular theme or topic

narrative a story, tale or any recital of events, and the manner in which it is told. First person narratives ('I') are told from the character's perspective and usually require the reader to judge carefully what is being said; second person narratives ('you') suggest the reader is part of the story; in third person narratives ('he', 'she', 'they') the narrator may be intrusive (continually commenting on the story), impersonal or **omniscient**. More than one style of narrative may be used in a text

narrator the voice telling the story or relating a sequence of events

omniscient narrator a narrator who uses the third person narrative and has a god-like knowledge of events and of the thoughts and feelings of the characters

paradox a seemingly absurd or self-contradictory statement that is or may be true

pastoral idealised representation of the countryside and the life of those who live there

patriarch, patriarchy The *Oxford English Dictionary* defines the word 'patriarch' as 'a male head or ancestor of any people, tribe, or family'; patriarchy is a social system of government in which power is held by elder males and passed to the younger males exclusively

personification the treatment or description of an object or an idea as human, with human attributes and feelings

point of view the 'eyes' through which we see the narrative action unfold, and thus the dominant narrative perspective within a text

propaganda communication with a message, which tries to persuade its audience to conform to a particular point of view or way of thinking

protagonist the principal character in a work of literature

realism a literary form that attempts to accurately imitate real life

reporting clause 'he said', 'she said', etc; providing the information regarding who is speaking in a conversation

satire a type of literature in which folly, evil or topical issues are held up to scorn through ridicule, irony or exaggeration

simile a figure of speech which compares two things using the words 'like' or 'as'

symbolism investing material objects with abstract powers and meanings greater then their own; allowing a complex idea to be represented by a single object

synonym a word that means the same or nearly the same as another word

tragedy in its original sense, a drama dealing with elevated actions and emotions and characters of high social standing in which a terrible outcome becomes inevitable as a result of an unstoppable sequence of events and a fatal flaw in the personality of the protagonist. More recently, tragedy has come to include courses of events happening to ordinary individuals that are inevitable because of social and cultural conditions or natural disasters

AUTHOR OF THESE NOTES

Sarah Gamble is Reader in English with Gender at Swansea University. She specialises in teaching and researching contemporary women's writing, and has published extensively on the life and works of Angela Carter.

GCSE

Maya Angelou
I Know Why the Caged Bird Sings

Jane Austen
Pride and Prejudice

Alan Ayckbourn
Absent Friends

Elizabeth Barrett Browning
Selected Poems

Robert Bolt
A Man for All Seasons

Harold Brighouse
Hobson's Choice

Charlotte Brontë
Jane Eyre

Emily Brontë
Wuthering Heights

Brian Clark
Whose Life is it Anyway?

Robert Cormier
Heroes

Shelagh Delaney
A Taste of Honey

Charles Dickens
David Copperfield
Great Expectations
Hard Times
Oliver Twist
Selected Stories

Roddy Doyle
Paddy Clarke Ha Ha Ha

George Eliot
Silas Marner
The Mill on the Floss

Anne Frank
The Diary of a Young Girl

William Golding
Lord of the Flies

Oliver Goldsmith
She Stoops to Conquer

Willis Hall
The Long and the Short and the Tall

Thomas Hardy
Far from the Madding Crowd
The Mayor of Casterbridge
Tess of the d'Urbervilles
The Withered Arm and other Wessex Tales

L. P. Hartley
The Go-Between

Seamus Heaney
Selected Poems

Susan Hill
I'm the King of the Castle

Barry Hines
A Kestrel for a Knave

Louise Lawrence
Children of the Dust

Harper Lee
To Kill a Mockingbird

Laurie Lee
Cider with Rosie

Arthur Miller
The Crucible
A View from the Bridge

Robert O'Brien
Z for Zachariah

Frank O'Connor
My Oedipus Complex and Other Stories

George Orwell
Animal Farm

J. B. Priestley
An Inspector Calls
When We Are Married

Willy Russell
Educating Rita
Our Day Out

J. D. Salinger
The Catcher in the Rye

William Shakespeare
Henry IV Part I
Henry V
Julius Caesar
Macbeth
The Merchant of Venice
A Midsummer Night's Dream
Much Ado About Nothing
Romeo and Juliet
The Tempest
Twelfth Night

George Bernard Shaw
Pygmalion

Mary Shelley
Frankenstein

R. C. Sherriff
Journey's End

Rukshana Smith
Salt on the Snow

John Steinbeck
Of Mice and Men

Robert Louis Stevenson
Dr Jekyll and Mr Hyde

Jonathan Swift
Gulliver's Travels

Robert Swindells
Daz 4 Zoe

Mildred D. Taylor
Roll of Thunder, Hear My Cry

Mark Twain
Huckleberry Finn

James Watson
Talking in Whispers

Edith Wharton
Ethan Frome

William Wordsworth
Selected Poems

A Choice of Poets

Mystery Stories of the Nineteenth Century including The Signalman

Nineteenth Century Short Stories

Poetry of the First World War

Six Women Poets

For the AQA Anthology:

Duffy and Armitage & Pre-1914 Poetry

Heaney and Clarke & Pre-1914 Poetry

Poems from Different Cultures

Key Stage 3

William Shakespeare
Much Ado About Nothing
Richard III
The Tempest

Margaret Atwood
Cat's Eye
The Handmaid's Tale
Jane Austen
Emma
Mansfield Park
Persuasion
Pride and Prejudice
Sense and Sensibility
Pat Barker
Regeneration
William Blake
Songs of Innocence and of Experience
The Brontës
Selected Poems
Charlotte Brontë
Jane Eyre
Villette
Emily Brontë
Wuthering Heights
Angela Carter
The Bloody Chamber
Nights at the Circus
Wise Children
Geoffrey Chaucer
The Franklin's Prologue and Tale
The Merchant's Prologue and Tale
The Miller's Prologue and Tale
The Prologue to the Canterbury Tales
The Pardoner's Tale
The Wife of Bath's Prologue and Tale
Caryl Churchill
Top Girls
John Clare
Selected Poems
Joseph Conrad
Heart of Darkness
Charles Dickens
Bleak House
Great Expectations
Hard Times
John Donne
Selected Poems
Carol Ann Duffy
Selected Poems
The World's Wife
George Eliot
Middlemarch
The Mill on the Floss
T. S. Eliot
Selected Poems
The Waste Land

Sebastian Faulks
Birdsong
F. Scott Fitzgerald
The Great Gatsby
John Ford
'Tis Pity She's a Whore
John Fowles
The French Lieutenant's Woman
Michael Frayn
Spies
Charles Frazier
Cold Mountain
Brian Friel
Making History
Translations
William Golding
The Spire
Thomas Hardy
Jude the Obscure
The Mayor of Casterbridge
The Return of the Native
Selected Poems
Tess of the d'Urbervilles
Nathaniel Hawthorne
The Scarlet Letter
Seamus Heaney
Selected Poems from 'Opened Ground'
Homer
The Iliad
The Odyssey
Khaled Hosseini
The Kite Runner
Aldous Huxley
Brave New World
Henrik Ibsen
A Doll's House
James Joyce
Dubliners
John Keats
Selected Poems
Philip Larkin
High Windows
The Whitsun Weddings and Selected Poems
Ian McEwan
Atonement
Christopher Marlowe
Doctor Faustus
Edward II
Arthur Miller
All My Sons
Death of a Salesman
John Milton
Paradise Lost Books I and II

George Orwell
Nineteen Eighty-Four
Sylvia Plath
Selected Poems
William Shakespeare
Antony and Cleopatra
As You Like It
Hamlet
Henry IV Part I
King Lear
Macbeth
Measure for Measure
The Merchant of Venice
A Midsummer Night's Dream
Much Ado About Nothing
Othello
Richard II
Richard III
Romeo and Juliet
The Taming of the Shrew
The Tempest
Twelfth Night
The Winter's Tale
Mary Shelley
Frankenstein
Richard Brinsley Sheridan
The School for Scandal
Bram Stoker
Dracula
Alfred Tennyson
Selected Poems
Virgil
The Aeneid
Alice Walker
The Color Purple
John Webster
The Duchess of Malfi
The White Devil
Oscar Wilde
The Importance of Being Earnest
The Picture of Dorian Gray
A Woman of No Importance
Tennessee Williams
Cat on a Hot Tin Roof
The Glass Menagerie
A Streetcar Named Desire
Jeanette Winterson
Oranges Are Not the Only Fruit
Virginia Woolf
To the Lighthouse
William Wordsworth
The Prelude and Selected Poems
Wordsworth and Coleridge
Lyrical Ballads
Poetry of the First World War